A Merry Little Christmas

Winning Stories from
Covenant's Short Fiction Contest

With a Bonus Story by
Anita Stansfield

Covenant Communications, Inc.

Published by Covenant Communications, Inc.
American Fork, Utah

Printed in the United States of America
First Printing: September 1996

01 00 99 98 97 96 10 9 8 7 6 5 4 3 2 1

ISBN 1-57734-027-2

Contents

OF SHEPHERDS & ANGELS

BY JANELLE BIDDINGER HYATT

A flash of red. Audrey caught a glimpse of it in the rush of the headlights. It registered in her tired mind as a scarlet blur before she turned her eyes back to the curtain of snow that forever opened before her windshield.

A pom-pom. That was her first impression—a puff of bright yarn. Audrey's thoughts worked their way around the incongruity of it. The hour was late; another two hours and Christmas would arrive. Although, in this dark hour surrounded by ice and silence, Audrey felt little good will toward men.

It seemed she'd been considering it for long minutes. But in the actual half-second that sped by, without willing it, her foot slammed on the brakes. The car came to a halt amid flying gravel, just yelling distance from the red blur.

The car spun in reverse along the silent highway, paralleling six-foot snowbanks. It settled to a stop, and Audrey saw the wall of snow had opened onto what she remembered was a small dirt road. There, in the shadow of the snowbanks, Audrey found herself looking through the window into the face of a boy. The red pom-

pommed ski hat was pulled snug, covering his ears, hair, and forehead, leaving a solemn face so uncomplicated it might have belonged to a newborn.

But the eyes, dark blue and eyelash-shaded. In this still hour, amid the dead calm of a Christmas Eve when everyone else in the world was cozied together in bough-draped rooms, Audrey looked into the eyes of lost faith.

For a moment, Audrey stared, her own feelings mirrored in that simple face. Then she shook her head, and her thoughts cleared. Why would a boy, maybe seven or eight years old at the most, be standing here in this cold isolation? The child's dark coat, its worn fur collar suggesting recent residence in a secondhand store, was little protection against the frigid air. His hands were shoved tight into the pockets, and when one escaped to brush a snowflake from an eyelash, she saw short, rounded fingers—solid farmer's hands. Chubby hands, she thought, like those she used to pattycake in games with her son.

Without glancing around, Audrey considered her surroundings. This was a stretch of road she'd driven nearly daily in the three years she'd lived in this mountain valley, just a quarter-hour drive from one of Utah's major cities. Rolling wheat fields lay on one side. On the other, the landscape dropped down through leafless clumps of scrub oak before meeting up with a large irrigation reservoir. If one discounted the wild skunks and the occasional placid cow, there was little living to speak of here. The nearest house must be at least two miles away, Audrey guessed.

The boy looked to be of farmer stock. Maybe from one of the valley's earth-working families whose pioneer ancestors had settled here. The once-rural spaces were more and more filled with new homes whose brick facades, gabled roofs, and arched windows bespoke an affluence still unaccustomed here—and, Audrey thought, at odds with the old-timers. No, this plain boy could not have strayed from one of those new, manicured homes.

Audrey jumped from the car, and within seconds was crouched before the boy, inspecting his face. From his vantage point a few inches above her, the boy's smooth face turned unsmilingly down to meet Audrey's eyes. Without thinking, she gently enclosed the boy's small, cold hand in her own gloved hand, rubbing softly.

"Shouldn't you be at home?" she asked, purposefully keeping her voice free of the disquiet this strange meeting had engendered. "It's Christmas Eve, you know."

The boy stared at her calmly. The news didn't seem to affect him. Audrey tried again. "What's your name? Mine's Audrey, and I live about five miles down this road."

There was no response, though the boy's brow seemed to furrow a bit. If it was possible, he looked even more serious.

"Where do you live?" Audrey could think of nothing but the importance of learning that information. But the boy remained silent. She stood up and glanced around anxiously. There'd be few cars at this hour, she knew. From across the lake, the lights of far-off homes blinked mockingly.

She was alone. The boy was alone. Audrey swallowed back the taste of helplessness that came up like bile. She did the only thing possible—opening the car's passenger door, she gently nudged him inside. Then she eased the car back onto the asphalt and, stilled ruled by indecision, moved slowly down the road.

The first house that rolled into view announced the Christmas season with colored lights. On the snowy lawn, a miniature sleigh was pulled by reindeer the size of Chihuahuas. But the porch light blazed—optimistically, it seemed to Audrey. She pulled in the driveway and hurried up the porch stairs. A woman answered, dressed in party clothes, her streaked blond hair bobbed perkily. In the background, shouts and laughter could be heard above the strains of "Jingle Bell Rock."

"Are you missing a little boy?" The words were out before Audrey realized how stupid they sounded. The woman took a step back. "I mean, I found this little boy on the road about two miles back. He's not hurt or anything, but he seems lost." Audrey gave up talking and offered her most pleading look.

"He's not ours, of course." The woman looked over Audrey's shoulder toward the car.

"Perhaps you know him," Audrey said and stepped aside so the woman could inspect the boy in the glow of the porch light. Nestled in the car seat, he looked smaller than Audrey's first impression back at the isolated snowbank.

"No, but then we don't know many of our neighbors, and people around here seem to keep to themselves," she answered. She paused in thought for a few seconds. "That's very strange. Why would a little boy be wandering around outside on Christmas Eve? I couldn't bribe mine to leave, what with Santa Claus and all."

"I know how it is," Audrey gave a polite laugh. "Thank you anyway."

"Do you need to use our phone or anything?" the woman called as Audrey turned away.

"No, thanks. I'll keep on looking."

Back in the car, Audrey gave the boy another searching inspection. She pulled off the hat to reveal straight hair, combed back from his forehead. In the dusk of the car, it appeared almost black. The nose, broad and splashed with freckles, anchored an open, roundish face. A face, Audrey thought, that probably looked most natural with an orange deer-hunting cap atop it and the grace of the sun upon it.

"Are you going to tell me your name?" she teased. She lifted his chin with her finger and his dark blue eyes met hers. "It's Christmas Eve, and you shouldn't be sitting here in a car with me. You should be home with your family. I bet your mom and dad are really worried." The boy looked back down at his lap, and Audrey sensed that the beginnings of a connection between them had been broken.

"Oh well, why don't you come home with me until we can find your own home," Audrey said with finality. In the gloom of the night, she and the boy headed toward home and uncertainty.

* * *

The old house was dark as Audrey pulled into the driveway. Christmas hadn't visited here yet, and Audrey felt a pang of regret that the house was not cheerier to welcome this somber young visitor.

The boy came willingly as Audrey led him from the garage through the back French doors into a dark family room. She flipped on the light, and the boy looked around without much curiosity at a drab Christmas tree that sheltered only a few carelessly thrown packages. Audrey bent to plug in the tree's lights, then turned to look at the boy. "Still not very cheerful, is it? I guess I haven't had much Christmas spirit this year. Maybe you can help me with that."

She motioned the boy to a couch and unzipped his coat. He offered no resistance as she pulled out one arm, then the other. "Sit here for a minute, okay?" Audrey left the room briefly, and came back with a phone, dialing as she walked.

"Tom, this is Audrey Merrill. Sorry to bother you on Christmas Eve," she said, then paused. "Yeah, I'm holding up okay. I worked the evening shift at the newspaper, and I'm just getting home." She smiled at the friendly sympathy in the voice of Tom Payne, a neighbor whose family often competed with hers for the back row of pews at church. But it was Tom's professional opinion that Audrey sought now. He was a sheriff's deputy, and Audrey hoped he could tell her what to do.

"Listen. Something weird has happened. On my way home from work just now, I came across a little boy on the road. He seems all right, just cold and lost. I didn't know what to do. I couldn't leave him there, so I brought him home with me." She gave him the details: The lonely, houseless stretch of road. A boy with chubby fingers and an unsmiling face, seven or eight at the most, just like her own son, Matthew. Not quite as tall, but with the same color of freckles.

"His name? That's the strange part. He won't talk. He won't tell me, and he won't tell me where he lives." Audrey paused. "Well, yes, I think he *can* talk." Audrey covered the phone and looked at the boy, sitting as still and tense as a fretful old man. "Are you hurt?" He shook his head without looking up. "You sure you won't tell me your name?"

There were a few seconds of silence, then a sound like an intake of breath. "Just a second, Tom." Andrey knelt down before the boy. "What, honey?"

"Mack." The boy's lowered head had not moved, and Audrey wasn't sure she'd heard right.

"Mack?" she coaxed. "As in, old MacDonald had a farm?" She said it in a gentle, singsong tone as she smoothed loose strands of hair from the boy's brow. He looked into her sympathetic, smiling eyes and nodded.

"Thank you," she whispered.

Into the phone she repeated, "Mack, his name is Mack." She listened. "I don't know Mack what. He's just not a talker."

Tom recited back the boy's description, then promised he'd call her as soon as he had any news. "Thanks, Tom," she said as she hung up the phone.

Audrey looked over the room, searching for some quick ways to add Christmas warmth. There weren't any, and she regretted for a moment that she'd worked so hard to reduce Christmas to nothing more than an inconvenience. She gently lifted Mack's chin and looked into his earnest eyes. "Would you like some hot chocolate, Mack? To me, it's just not Christmas Eve without a cup of hot chocolate." The boy's silence seemed to her a quiet consent.

* * *

Outside, the moon made its easy way across the sky, nodding to any number of blinking beacons that might have been the Christmas star. Audrey smothered a hollowness in her throat that threatened to overwhelm her. She glanced in her chocolate mug at the cold remains, and sat the mug down, turning away from the window.

From the far corner, the Christmas tree's lights cast a happy, muted light, too dim to overshadow the gleam of moon on snow. And for the hundredth time that evening, she wished the certainty of daylight would arrive, drying up regrets like a dripping pair of children's swimming trunks slung over the deck to catch the summer sun. It was too easy to get lost in that odd jewel light, blinking green, now red and blue. The wry thought came to Audrey that Christmas lights reflected moods—to those who welcomed Christmas, snug in the arms of family, the bulbs glowed a quiet, embracing welcome. To all others, the lights blinked all the colors of loss.

A rustle of movement awoke Audrey from her reverie, and in a fleeting moment of forgetfulness she looked upon the boy, Mack, with surprise. "Oops. Caught me thinking," she smiled. "Maybe thinking too hard." The boy sat on the edge of the sofa, knees primly locked together, his hands wrapped around his chocolate mug as if it were a buoy. There was a calm dignity about him, although his shoulders were pulled inward in a pose of surrender. Audrey could make out the image on his sweatshirt's front; it was of the Masters of the Universe cartoon that Audrey remembered had been popular a few years back. Her own son had giggled uproariously when he'd unwrapped a present, back on a Christmas when the lights had blinked only warmth, to reveal a bubble bath jar in the hero's muscled shape. On Mack, the sweatshirt's too-short sleeves revealed tender swatches of wrist. Audrey thought the knee-faded jeans were probably from the same era, too short as well.

The telephone bell jangled a sharp note. When Audrey answered it, Tom's voice on the line reminded her of the incongruity of this little boy lost before her. She braced for the flash of disappointment she knew would follow when Tom's professional voice snipped away all the mystery of this Christmas visitor.

Instead, Tom let go a drawling, thoughtful "Welllll. I don't know what to tell you, Audrey. No one's heard peep one about a missing boy. County dispatch hasn't taken any calls, and I've checked with all the surrounding cities. Nothing. Looks like you've found yourself a true Christmas puzzle."

Audrey glanced at the quiet boy, who was fidgeting with his mug, seemingly unaware he was being discussed. She was unsure what to say. "So, what should I do, Tom?"

"If you can just hang tight for a bit, we'll send a deputy out to pick up the boy. Can you entertain him for a half hour or so?" Tom asked.

"What will happen to him then?"

"I don't know. We'll find a place for him until we can get this figured out."

"So," Audrey's mind was racing, "he'll spend Christmas Eve at the station?"

"Yes, looks that way."

For the second time that evening, Audrey heard herself speaking as if she was a spectator, not willing the words. The first time had been on that dark stretch of road, when she had coaxed the boy from the black of night into the shelter of her car. Now, her voice carried the same calm authority. "Well, can't he just stay here? I'd love to have somebody to sing a few Christmas carols with." Audrey glanced at Mack, and this time he was looking at her searchingly. "You can just call me when you find out something, okay? There doesn't seem to be any need for him to just sit around in some dingy police waiting room."

"Hey," Tom laughed. "I don't know what you're talking about. I work in the lap of luxury here. We've got carpet and a coffee maker. Hey, we've even got a Christmas tree with lights that work—if you jiggle the plug just right." Audrey gave a polite laugh, and felt some of the tightness leave her shoulders. "Well, I don't see any harm in that," Tom continued. "But how's he going to sing when he won't even talk?"

"Oh, maybe he'll just hum." Audrey sat on the couch alongside the boy and curved her arm protectively around his shoulders. "The spirit's in the music, you know, not in the way it's sung."

*   *   *

Audrey flipped on the lights, consigning away memories with the dark. She headed to the kitchen to make a Christmas Eve dinner of grilled cheese sandwiches. Midway, she stopped and turned back to Mack. "We need some Christmas music, don't we?"

Mack said nothing. But Audrey kept up a stream of conversation as she walked to the coat closet and pulled from its depths a brown cardboard box. "Here's my Christmas collection. They're mostly records. Everyone's gone to CDs now, but I just can't find it in me to get rid of all these classics." She planted the box at Mack's feet and pulled out an album with the cheerful face of Tony Bennett. "Bet you haven't heard of him," she chattered on. "He's a little before my time, too, but I remember my mom playing his records."

Elvis Presley and Anne Murray were pulled from the box and joined the pile of Christmas albums, along with Alvin and the Chipmunks and the Oakridge Boys. "You look and see if there's anything you want to hear," Audrey said, drawing Mack down on the floor. "And while you're doing that, I'll put this one on." She fiddled with the phonograph, and soon Bing Crosby was promising to be home for Christmas. She wished briefly she'd chosen a carol less in tune with her mood.

Soon Bing was on to Christmas in Killarney, and Audrey, buttering bread and cutting cheese, sensed that the house had warmed up to their presence—and perhaps, she thought, to Christmas. It was as if the house itself had a void that matched the one in her heart. She shook off the thought that the old structure, which had protected several generations of families, seemed to miss the presence of the children—its own children—just as she did.

She spread the sandwiches and milk on the floor before the gas fireplace and motioned Mack to join her. He silently settled down crosslegged and accepted a sandwich.

"You know, that whole idea of the silent leading man only works in the movies," Audrey teased. "We're stuck here for the evening, so we might as well be friends." Mack looked up briefly from his sandwich, and she marveled at the clearness of his blue eyes, set wide on his round face. She felt some of the tension ease away.

"Are you lonely?" Audrey probed gently. "Do you miss your family? Your mom?" Mack's eyebrows furrowed, and Audrey watched his face close in upon itself. She moved away from that sensitive area.

"I have a son about your age. In fact, you remind me a lot of him," Audrey said. "He's got freckles kind of like yours, and his eyes are blue too. How old are you? Seven?" Mack gave an almost imperceptible nod.

"Matthew—that's my son's name—just turned eight. We call him our monster, because his birthday's on Halloween." Audrey gave a soft laugh that settled into a sigh. She saw the unspoken question on Mack's face. "He's not here right now, because he's with his dad." Mack's face still questioned. "His dad doesn't live here anymore." She gestured toward a collection of framed photographs above them on the mantel. Both looked up, Mack with a hint of curiosity, Audrey with sorrow.

"That's Matthew's sister, Rachel. She's five." Audrey paused. Rachel, a precocious kindergartner who'd organized her dolls into casts for dramatic reenactments of her favorite movies, who couldn't sleep without her Pooh bear cuddled beneath the covers and her mother singing "My Favorite Things" in the quiet closeness of her dark bedroom. The pink baby girl who should have been satisfied with the glossy brown hair of her mother, but who defied genetics to enter the world with a mass of independent golden curls.

"I miss them terribly." Audrey gave up talking and concentrated on finishing the now-tasteless sandwich. By all that was right in heaven, Audrey thought, she should not be alone on this night of all that the year offered. It was as if her big present, the one that teased in its beribboned beauty, had been taken away from her. It was unnatural, she told herself—unnatural and unfair to have this stolen from her.

Inside, the ache Audrey had tried to suppress threatened to close in upon her. She'd pushed Christmas away, packing up presents and Santa Claus decorations as she'd packed her children's suitcases. She didn't want Christmas, and though she'd decked a holiday home in the first weeks of December, putting on a cheerful, anticipatory face for her children, all was now bundled and boxed away. No need of it now, since Matthew and Rachel wouldn't be back until after New Year's.

She'd lost all this by default. There had been no blowout, no battle, just an ebbing away of her relationship with her husband, Paul. It had seemed almost comfortable at the time.

Rachel's move into preschool and now kindergarten had allowed Audrey to return to her former profession of journalism. She'd found herself working as many hard hours as the young college graduates with whom she competed for assignments. The relentless pace, the influence she carried as a reporter—all of it began to seem more real and vital than her marriage. In the newsroom, everything mattered; *she* mattered. And it was intoxicating.

Paul's career as a computer programmer for a chain of hospitals pulled him away from home more and more. He was gone weekends, and there'd be days following days that Audrey didn't see him. He'd joked once that he spent more time sleeping in airports than in his own bed.

And so, when Paul learned he was being transferred to San Francisco, Audrey declined to go. She had her job, the children were doing well in school, she'd furnished their old home with care and attention. It seemed too great a sacrifice to give all of that up.

Paul was hurt and perplexed. Audrey explained that her love must have dried up, worn out, she didn't know what. And when the awful realization settled in that his wife had chosen the life she'd created over a future with her husband, he had simply withdrawn in sullen defeat. Close-faced and silently angry, he'd left, taking with him only the promise of having his children with him at

Christmas and for a portion of the summer.

It was all gone before she'd realized it, like chill dew that if not touched with bare feet on a summer morning and relished for its cool purity, evaporated in the afternoon warmth. One didn't notice the dew dissolving; it dried away and was gone, leaving only the summer heat.

Audrey sat without moving, wreathed in grief and regret. Then, unobtrusively, ever so quietly, she felt a small hand creep into hers.

* * *

Audrey gave a shake of her head and became aware of the room, carefully decorated over the years to reflect her young family. The Christmas tree and Bing's voice filled the room with warmth and color. And before her sat a small boy, his feet tucked out of sight, a milk moustache gracing his upper lip.

Rail against Christmas all she might, it was here around her. It was present in the off-step dance of the red and blue bulbs; in the anticipation that hung in the air like the scent of fresh fir boughs; in this small child. And Audrey surrendered to it.

"Does it seem like Christmas to you, Mack?" Audrey gently held the boy's hand and waited for a response. When there was none, she continued, "There are a few things I do to celebrate Christmas, and they're very important to me. We've had our hot chocolate; that's one. If my children were here with me, we'd read the Christmas story. Do you mind if I read it?"

Mack shook his head. Audrey pulled the family

Bible from the bottom shelf of a nearby lamp table. Like countless times before, the white embossed cover gave Audrey a ripple of rich memory as she ran her palm over it. She and Mack settled side by side on the couch, the leather volume on her lap.

The Bible opened to embellished front plates, with gold flourishes and bright colors mimicking the illustrations done by monks of old. There were the names of her parents, who had presented the Bible to her and Paul on their wedding day. Paul's name was linked in elegant calligraphy with her own, and Audrey's finger traced down the page to the names of Matthew and Rachel.

Audrey paused to smile at the names before her. She felt their love and, it seemed for a moment, their presence. She hadn't lost them, she knew in her heart; their bonds were too strong to be weakened by mere absence.

The boy nestled almost imperceptibly closer; Audrey sensed it more than felt the physical movement. She pulled him close with an embracing arm.

"Do you know the story of Jesus' birth?" Audrey asked, and Mack gave a brief nod. "Let's begin here in Luke." Audrey found the page and began reading the familiar lines. "'And it came to pass in those days, that there went out a decree from Caesar Augustus, that all the world should be taxed. And all went to be taxed, every one into his own city.'"

The words and rhythms washed over Audrey like the soft, comforting kisses of so many angels. She read on, her finger moving caressingly from verse to verse. She spoke the words, but she was no longer reading. Countless Christmas retellings had tied the story to her heart as securely as were her children's names. "'And she brought forth her firstborn son and wrapped him in swaddling clothes and laid him in a manger, because there was no room for him in the inn.'"

A slight movement caught Audrey mid-sentence, and she raised her hand from the Bible page to Mack's cheek. "Are you okay, honey?" she asked. Again the boy offered his mute nod, and she turned her eyes back to the simple tale. "'And there were in the same country shepherds abiding in the field, keeping watch over their flock by night.'"

"Shepherd." The word came so quietly and unexpectedly that Audrey's next words snagged in her throat.

"Did you say something, Mack?" she leaned closer.

"Shepherd. My dad told me he was a shepherd, only that's not what they call them anymore." After Mack's silence, this flood of words washed away Audrey's composure for a moment.

"He's, what, a rancher? Sheepherder?" Audrey peered intently into the little face.

"Yeah, but he's gone. My grandma says he lives with the angels now."

Audrey felt the warmth of a tear on her arm wrapped around the boy's chest, and then she was conscious of the quiver of a muffled sob. "Sweetheart, I'm so sorry," she began, but soon understood that her words had little meaning for him.

"Look, it talks more about shepherds here. Shepherds were the only people the angels invited to the stable to see the baby Jesus. The three wise men came later, but the shepherds were there first. They were very special people—very lucky people," Audrey said quietly. Mack's shoulders relaxed slightly as she continued. "See, the angels were so happy when Jesus was born that they were celebrating, lighting up the sky with their music and excitement, and the shepherds saw them. The story goes: 'And lo, the angel of the Lord came upon them,'— came upon the shepherds who were out tending their sheep," she added in an aside, "'and the glory of the Lord shone round about them; and they were sore afraid. And the angel said unto them, Fear not; for behold, I bring you good tidings of great joy, which shall be to all people.'

"Great joy. Do you know what that feels like?" Audrey asked. "I think it must be how your daddy felt when you were born. When I held my little ones in my arms for the first time, that's what I felt. And I know that your daddy's watching over you, just like an angel, and wishing he could hold you in his arms." She hugged him tighter. "You still bring him great joy, Mack. Every day."

They sat that way, unmoving, for the space of several moments. Then Audrey brushed flat the thin page of the Bible. "This is what the angels told the shepherds: 'For unto you is born this day in the city of David a Saviour, which is Christ the Lord. And this shall be a sign unto you; ye shall find the baby wrapped in swaddling clothes, lying in a manger.'

"'And suddenly there was with the angel a multitude of the heavenly host praising God, and saying, Glory to God in the highest, and on earth peace, good will toward men.'"

Audrey closed the Bible and set it on the floor. "I think that's my favorite story. I've probably heard it a thousand times, but every time it's still like opening a gift." Mack nodded and nestled his head beneath her arm.

"Mack," Audrey asked tentatively, "is your grandma close by? Do you want to call her?"

"No, I want to stay here."

Audrey leaned back into the soft crook of the couch, pulling Mack with her. She rocked him gently, and the slight body released the last of its tensions. "You know, you are an angel, Mack," she whispered in his ear. "You're my Christmas angel."

Audrey held him as he fell asleep under the calming sheen of the Christmas lights. For an hour she remained motionless, absorbing the boy's smell, forming rings with his hair, soothed by the rhythm of his regular breathing. She thought of the Christmas Eves she had known, joyful times of anticipation and reverence. She saw her children in their Christmas pajamas, the red and green ribbons from the just-opened boxes exuberantly draped around necks and wrists, Paul laughing as he snapped photographs. She thought of her own childhood, when the final task before bedtime was to prepare a plate of cookies for Santa. For her, and later for her children, it was a small but necessary gift whose omission would upset the balance of things hoped for and things received.

Audrey started, and a twinge of panic shivered through her. How, she thought, could she have forgotten the cookies? Had she become so lost in her own grief that she'd overlooked this, the most simple offering of the season?

The silence was broken only by the boy's regular breathing as Audrey tenderly settled him on the couch. She stacked up the dishes from their dinner and busied herself with a few late-night tasks.

Christmas Eve had given way to Christmas morning when Audrey returned to the couch. She squeezed alongside Mack's sleepy frame, arranging her feet on the coffee table. His head moved in sleep to that sheltering place between mother's arm and breast that a child instinctively seeks. To Audrey, Mack's warm body was like a balm. She pulled him closer, and, with one last weary blink that acknowledged good will toward men—and children—she slept.

* * *

The sun woke Audrey as it splashed through the room's large window, competing for attention with the glowing bulbs of the Christmas tree. Mack stirred too, and sat straight-backed, blinking in the sunlight. He felt Audrey's hand smooth his hair, and he turned toward her. A smile scattered the freckles, and Audrey saw a hint of the mischievousness and spunk that had been muted by the boy's suffering.

"Merry Christmas, Mack," she said brightly. "Do you want some orange juice?" He nodded, and she pulled him from the couch, clasping his hand.

Standing and shaking sleep from his eyes, Mack nearly tripped over the gift-wrapped box sitting just a puppy's leap from his feet. It was about the size of a milk crate and was topped with a red bow nearly as big as a dinner plate. A tag hung loosely from the bow, its inscription so clear that Mack could read it without bending down: "To Mack, the mystery boy. Merry Christmas."

With a squeal, Mack fell to his knees and reached for the bow. He jerked his hand back, and turned questioningly to Audrey. At her smile and nod, he turned back to the box. He gazed at the red present for three or four heartbeats, then, in a flurry of motion, tore at the wrapping until he was surrounded by loose paper and ribbon. Seconds later, Mack stood triumphant, carefully holding a gleaming red dump truck with both hands.

"Is this from Santa?" Mack asked. The boy hardly paused from his intense examination of opening doors and lifting the truck's bed to ask the question.

"It must be," answered Audrey, who was now kneeling nearby. "I think he's been here, because look . . ." At the surprise in her voice, Mack looked sharply to where she pointed. A small plate sat on the table. All that was on it were crumbs of what had just hours earlier been stale vanilla wafers, the only cookies Audrey could find.

Audrey gave a chuckle, paused for a moment, then laughed out loud. It was a laugh of release, celebration, and forgiveness. Mack joined in with a tentative titter that ripened into a rush of childish giggles. And so it was that Tom found them, the woman and boy kneeling before the Christmas tree, arms around each other, laughing as if their hearts would break.

At the sound of the knock, Audrey and Mack turned

to the front door to see Tom peering in, his shoulders hunched against the cold. She opened the door and Tom stepped in, bringing a splash of light and chill with him. "Merry Christmas, Audrey," he grinned. Then he looked at Mack. "So this is the Christmas puzzle," he said, sitting down on his haunches so he was eye to eye with the youngster. He looked up at Audrey. "Have you solved him yet?"

"Mack doesn't need solving," she answered. "He's got all the pieces right there. He knows the answers, and that's what's important."

"Perhaps," said Tom.

"We were reading the Christmas story last evening, and I came across a scripture that reminded me of Mack. It's a description of Jesus as a young boy. 'The child grew,'" Audrey quoted from memory, "'and waxed strong in spirit, filled with wisdom; and the grace of God was upon him.' Mack has that gift, the grace of God." She took Mack's hand in hers. "So, Tom, any news on Mack's family?"

"Well, yes. This morning we heard from the boy's grandmother. She's out in the car." Tom was still on eye-level with Mack, and his voice was compassionate. "The boy's mother's been gone since he was just a babe. Mack's father died a few months back. Since then, his grandma says, he's been taken by some kind of grief. He's pretty much stopped talking, and he's run away several times. Last night, I guess, the Christmas preparations were too much for him."

Tom paused for a moment. "His grandma lives on a farm near the lake; she'd been up most of the night before she called us this morning. Mack must have traveled four or five miles last night before you found him."

"No," Audrey said, "I think he found me."

"Anyway, hold on while I go get Mrs. Anderson." Tom was gone in a gust of cold air. Audrey knelt and took Mack's hands gently in her own. She stopped to compose herself, blinking back inconvenient tears. "Mack, I am so sorry for your loss." She gently kissed the tops of his hands. "I want to thank you. You saved me this Christmas, you know. Here you are, the person who needed help, and instead you helped me. 'Blessed are they that mourn, for they shall be comforted.' Jesus said that. And you blessed me, just by being here. You have a big spirit and a loving heart. Those will help you through this."

She gave Mack a quick squeeze, then opened the door to admit Tom and the older woman. Mrs. Anderson was tall and straight, her body lean from a life of working the earth. Her steel-gray hair was held in a thick, girlish braid that reached down her back, but her no-nonsense face spoke of countless mornings under an unforgiving sun and as many afternoons over a steamy stove.

Her face softened as she lifted Mack off the floor into her arms. She didn't speak, but merely held the boy tight. Mack's arms went around her, and he buried his face in her neck. As sobs shook his body, his grandmother stood solid and unmoving.

Audrey and Tom waited, too. Several minutes passed before Mack quieted, and Mrs. Anderson set him down. "I'm sorry, Grandma," Mack's voice quivered. "I didn't want to hurt your feelings. I just missed Dad so much."

"I know," his grandmother answered, taking his face in her hands. "But I want you to come home with me now, okay?" Mack nodded and again reached for the comfort of her arms. Her response was quick and tender, and Audrey sensed the strong bond between the grandmother and boy. The woman's love reached out and encircled the boy like a soft blanket.

Audrey realized that as her friendship with Mack had deepened through the evening hours, so had her apprehension. Why was Mack running? What had he left behind? Unconsciously, she had assembled in her mind a picture of a lonely home life, bereft of love. But now, as she watched the two of them, she understood in her heart that Mack would be fine.

The older woman stood to face Audrey, still holding Mack's hand in hers. "Your name is Audrey Merrill?" Audrey nodded. "I give you my thanks for providing shelter to my grandson last night."

Audrey blushed and shook her head. "No, the pleasure was mine. I would have spent the evening alone, and Mack gave me . . . well," she searched for the word, and finally chose a phrase she knew was inadequate, "much-needed company."

Mrs. Anderson nodded in understanding. "My son Will, Mack's father, died last fall from a cancer that moved so fast we didn't have time to prepare. He was fine, working on the farm, and one day just collapsed. He never regained consciousness fully. And Mack and I are still in shock."

She pulled Mack closer. "But we still have each

other. Isn't that right, son?" The boy nodded. "And Mack knows his daddy loves him, that he's got his own special guardian angel. This Christmas the hurt was too fresh," Mrs. Anderson was now speaking directly to Mack. "But he's with us here," she tapped Mack's chest. "And he'll be with us at every Christmas, and every night when we go to sleep, and every morning when we say our prayers."

"I know," Mack said thoughtfully. Then he looked up with a hopeful smile. "Grandma, I think he'd like Audrey, don't you?"

Mrs. Anderson smiled, and clasping Audrey's hand in both of hers, turned toward the door. "Wait," Audrey cried, and ran to the closet. Umbrellas and board games tumbled down before she pulled out a Polaroid camera. "I want a picture of my Christmas angel, okay?"

Mack moved to an easy pose, arms folded across his chest, a slight grin playing on his features. Audrey snapped the picture, and, setting the camera aside, gathered Mack into her arms for one last quick hug. "Do you think you might come over sometime and play with my Matthew?" she asked the boy. "I think you two could be good friends."

Her last impression of Mack that Christmas Day was not of the lost waif she had found wandering along the road. This boy, walking in step with his grandmother down the front stoop, carried his thin, sharp shoulders upright—almost, Audrey thought, in a stance of dignity. Mack, holding tight the red dump truck, turned to wave. Then he was gone around the side of the house.

Audrey returned to the protection of the house. This

time, the Christmas tree lights blinked in greeting, and Audrey smiled at the welcoming warmth of the fireplace. She sat in front of the flames and let them play around her thoughts, seeing in them the beloved faces of her children. This time, when the memories knocked softly, Audrey invited them in and was surrounded by the consoling images of Christmases past, as well as yet-unknown Christmases she knew the years ahead promised.

The telephone's ring drew her attention from the flames. Over the receiver, her children's high voices rang with excitement, but there was a note of apprehension. "Hi, Mom," Matthew squeaked. "Merry Christmas." Then, "Are you okay?"

"Yes, I am," Audrey laughed. "Tell me about your Christmas." And so they did, in a rush of words Audrey didn't even try to sort out.

Then their squeals were replaced with the calm voice of her husband, Paul. "Hello, Audrey." Her throat pinched shut as if a hand had clasped it. No words would come. "Are you there?" Paul asked, and she was warmed by the overtones of concern in his voice.

"Yes."

"Audrey, we need to talk, okay?"

"Oh, Paul, I'm so sorry. This has all been my fault." Then she stopped. These words of anguish and regret didn't seem fit companions to a Christmas morning.

"The kids were supposed to fly home a week from tomorrow," Paul's voice filled the void. "I think I'll fly back with them tomorrow instead. Then maybe we can . . . well . . . talk about this. Is that okay with you?"

"Yes, I'll be here." Audrey moved to hang up the phone, then she paused. "Paul?"

"Yes?"

"I miss you this Christmas."

"Thank you, Audrey. See you soon."

Audrey stood next to the now-silent phone, her hand tightly covering her mouth. A ripple of emotion gripped her, and she was unsure whether, if she relaxed enough to make a sound, it would be a laugh or a cry.

The Christmas tree drew her back into the living room, and she stood in its glow, sorting through her thoughts. She had many preparations to make and only a few hours. There was food to buy, meals to plan for her family. Christmas, she thought, needed to be invited back. But for now it was enough to consult with the Christmas tree, standing patiently in its elegant costume like an old companion that had long been neglected.

Audrey found the Polaroid photo of Mack; from its square confines he looked up at her, pleased and at peace. She carried the photograph to the fireplace mantel and carefully placed it among the images of her son and daughter.

Just then, a flash of red caught her eye. Tucked in the cushion of the couch, she saw the red knitted cap. She pulled it out, caressing the worn pom-pom, and it too was placed on the mantel alongside the photograph. Here, in the glow of the Christmas tree and fireplace, the cap added a cheerful splash of holiday red—a welcome splash of memory.

"Merry Christmas, Mack," she whispered. "And thank you."

About the Author

Janelle Biddinger Hyatt holds a degree in communications from the University of Utah and is currently attending Weber State University to obtain a teaching certificate to teach journalism on a high school level. She has been a news/feature writer and editor for a number of newspapers, and has received several awards for her work.

Janelle lives with her husband, Rodney, and three children in Eden, Utah.

THE TINIEST STOCKING

BY ALICE MORREY BAILEY

"After the baby comes, will we keep Margaret?"

Daddy's voice came suddenly, sharp and clear, from the other room. Margaret, munching a cookie and reading the comics in the paper that lined a drawer in the pantry, was not supposed to hear this. Her hand stopped halfway to her mouth, waiting in sudden fear for Mother's answer. Not her real parents, she reminded herself, because she was a foster child from County Welfare.

"I hadn't thought about it," Mother finally said. "Why, she's been with us so long—nearly three years now."

So long that Margaret had begun to feel that this home was her very own, that Mother and Daddy were real, not foster, and Richie and Davy were her own little brothers. It had been different from the start, like coming to a place she already knew. Like coming home.

She had come up the walk with Miss Billings, the case worker who always took her and brought her back from the homes she had lived in, seven of them as far back as she could remember. This time was different from all the others. She liked everything from the first. It was like coming into Fairyland, the white cottage with the white picket fence, silver icicles hanging from the eaves, holly bushes, the hooded trees, yellow shutters, snowy flounces of curtains crisscrossing the big window. The walk was of red stones, the blue roof peeked through by the chimney.

When they entered the house there were Mother and Richard, who was then almost three, and little David, only six months old, kicking and gooing in the bassinet. And Daddy, sitting back a little, but watching.

"Here's your new little girl," Miss Billings had said. "Her name is Margaret."

Mother had held out her hands, drawing Margaret near to her. She hadn't said a word, but looked right into Margaret's eyes, and Margaret had searched her face. There was that mother look in her eyes, that look of understanding and caring and loving. And then she held Margaret close. Margaret pressed her face against Mother, and it was like she had traveled a long time through a scary night and had reached home where everything was safe at last.

Mother spoke, jerking Margaret back into the fearful now. "I want to be fair to you, though, Michael. You work so very hard making a living for us, and I don't want anything to be a burden to you. The welfare money—"

"Oh," Michael interrupted, "the welfare money is enough. They take care of her dental and medical bills if we need them, and clothes. I didn't want to make any money on her. I was thinking of the extra work for you.

Don't think I can't see you're not as well with this baby as you were with the others, and the doctor says you have to take it easier. Four kids to cook and sew and wash for—good heavens!"

"My mother had eight," Mother said quietly.

"I know, but I thought if the baby's a girl, it would kind of fill that need you've always had for a daughter."

"If the baby's a girl—" Mother said softly as if she were dreaming, "if the baby's a girl—"

Margaret could stand no more. She tiptoed out, closed the screen door carefully, and ran to hide and sob in the little thicket of currant bushes behind the house. It was there that Richie found her. She could see his sturdy little legs through her fingers.

"Did a bee bite you, Moggy?" he said.

"I'm laughing," said Margaret, thinking fast. "A bee tried to get into the little blossoms and fell off." One really had.

"Does laughing make tears in your eyes?" asked Richie, not convinced, so Margaret had to turn her crying to laughing until he laughed, too, and went running to tell Mother and Daddy. Davy caught the joke, and there were demonstrations of a bee falling off the tiny currant flower.

Afterward, Margaret watched Daddy to see if he had changed toward her, but he seemed the same as always, sometimes teasing her and calling her Molly, his eyes dancing. And she helped Mother every way she could—folding pillowcases, lifting Davy, and keeping Richie out of mischief every minute she was home from school. She learned new things, putting the clothes in the washer and taking them out of the dryer so Mother wouldn't have to go up and down the basement steps. She had lost one mother because of being sick, but most of them because of their moving away.

She had loved all of them, and had cried when she lost them, but she loved Mother most of all. Daddy called her "Colleen," and said her blue eyes and black hair came straight from Killarney. Mother said Daddy was Irish as Pat and Mike with his red hair and his temper. Only that was a joke, because Daddy always talked like his mouth was lined with cotton, especially to Mother.

Twice since June, Miss Billings had come to visit and nothing had happened. Of course, Margaret figured they were waiting to see if the baby was a girl. It wasn't as if Margaret wouldn't just love a baby girl; but then, of course, they wouldn't need her. That feeling turned her insides to jelly. Now it was Christmas time again.

Daddy had planned the traditional Christmas Eve drive through "Christmas Tree Lane" as much for Margaret, even though she was nine, as for the little children. When the car turned onto the street, Mother caught her breath in surprised wonder at the dazzling decorations.

"See! Pretty lights, Moggy," cried Davy, his blue eyes inches from her own. Putting his fat little hands on her cheeks, he turned her head to make her see. Margaret laughed in spite of the sadness inside.

"Margaret, are those boys too much for you?" asked Mother. "One of them better come in front with me."

"No!" Davy said with finality. "I stay Moggy."

"We want to stay with our sister," Richie added.

Their words made Margaret's heart swell up like a toasting marshmallow and go all spongy inside. "They're all right," she said, giving each of them a bear hug. Suddenly everything seemed all right. She was just like any nine-year-old with little brothers and a mother and father.

"Santa Claus will come tonight—down the chimney and fill up our stockings, won't he, Mama?" Mother didn't answer even when Richie kept asking her.

"We'll hang up our stockings in front of the fireplace, and he'll really and truly come," Margaret assured him.

"And fill them with toys," added Richie, his eyes dark with excitement.

"And candy and nuts," added Daddy. "And trim the tree."

"Yes," said Margaret, keeping the secret she knew about Santa Claus. A girl at school had told her last year, just before Christmas. She had thought then that Christmas would never be fun again, but Mother understood, and had her help with everything, and it had been even more fun.

This year she knew what the boys were getting, and where the gifts were hidden. She had been trusted with the secrets, and she was proud that she had kept them all. This year was different, though. There were fewer things because the baby was coming, and there were hospital and doctor bills and the layette. Besides, Mother was sick a lot. Sometimes Margaret saw Daddy looking at Mother with concern in his eyes, and it made a sharp fear in her.

"Angels sing up a'ky," Davy commented.

"What, Davy?" asked Daddy. No one but Margaret could understand him sometimes.

"He says the angels were singing up in the sky," Margaret interpreted. "Mother told us the story about it—the shepherds and the little baby Jesus, and the angels singing."

"That wasn't angels singing," said Richie scornfully. "They played the songs with a loudspeaker on top of the buildings, didn't they, Margaret?" There was no doubt that Davy and Richie were the two smartest little boys in the world.

When they arrived home, Margaret helped the boys out before she saw that something was wrong. Mother was out of the car, but she was just standing, leaning on Daddy.

"How long has this been going on?" Daddy asked in his tenderest voice.

"About an hour—before we went downtown."

"Why didn't you say something?" This time Daddy sounded almost angry.

"I didn't want to disappoint the children."

"Colleen, darling. You know what the doctor said!"

"I know, but I hoped this was a false alarm. Oh, Mike! This'll spoil Christmas for everybody!"

"It'll spoil life for everybody if you—" Daddy began, and stopped. Mother could move now.

"Thank goodness I got the laundry done," said Mother, "and my hair washed."

"That's just like a woman," Daddy grinned, but his

34

lips looked tight.

In the house, Mother sat heavily in a chair. She was trying to get Davy out of his snowsuit, but she had to stop and wait, resting her forehead on one hand. Daddy was at the phone, his big fingers jabbing at the dial, his heavy brows knitted.

"I can get them into bed, Mother," Margaret offered.

"If you only would!" Mother said without looking at Margaret, and let her take Davy. Richie, struggling manfully with his galoshes, wouldn't let her help him. As Margaret led them to the bedroom, Daddy's voice lifted as he made the connection.

"Hello? Is Dr. Barton in?"

"You'd better get ready for bed yourself, Margaret," Mother called after her.

Weren't they going to hang up their stockings? What about Christmas Eve? "But, Mother—" she began.

"Do as your mother says, Margaret! Get those boys into bed," Daddy said sharply.

Daddy had never spoken to her like that. Richie and Davy looked at him with round, frightened eyes, and tears stung Margaret's eyelids. She helped the boys get into their sleepers and say their prayers and then got on her own nightgown and slippers. She said her little prayer, but this time she didn't ask to be adopted.

"Please, Heavenly Father, let the baby be a boy. I'll help Mother all I can. I'll practice stirring the mush without lumping, and I'll sew on buttons. I won't take the dollar she gives me from the welfare money, and I'll keep my clothes clean if I can stay."

When she went to the bathroom to brush her teeth, Daddy was still at the telephone, his eyes frantic.

"Well, for Pete's sake! I can't get that baby-sitter, Colleen. The doctor wants you to come right to the hospital. He says it's urgent. So what do we do now? There's no one to leave the children with."

"Daddy," said Margaret, going to him. "I know the baby's coming and Mother has to go to the hospital. I can take care of Davy and Richie."

Daddy looked at her in astonishment. "No, I don't think so. You're too little."

"No I'm not. Truly I'm not. I know how to make beds and wash dishes and sweep. I can even cook, except mush without lumps. I can do it."

Daddy wavered with indecision. "What do you think, darling?"

But something had happened to Mother. She was lying on the couch, shaking violently, her teeth chattering. Daddy grabbed her up and made for the door, his eyes wild and desperate.

Margaret had to run after him with the little bag Mother had packed, out into the snow in her thin slippers. Neither of them waved goodbye, and their going left a great, aching emptiness.

Margaret shuffled slowly back into the living room, thinking heavily, a feeling of panic beating up in her. Daddy wasn't mad at her when he left. He was afraid! The things he said, the way Mother looked, the shaking, what the doctor said—it all added up to an awful fear. Was Mother going to die?

Margaret sat on the sofa, where the air was heavy

with the scent of the untrimmed Christmas tree, and felt great sobs forming deep down inside. She slipped to her knees and buried her head in the cushion, praying as hard as she could.

"Let Mother live, Heavenly Father. Don't let her die!" She strained as hard as she could to make Him hear, but she felt so small and unimportant. "If you'll let Mother live, I'll let the baby be a girl," she promised. "I'll go back to Miss Billings, and I won't even cry!"

She felt better then. It was such a big promise, the Lord must have heard. When she got to her feet, Davy and Richie were standing in the doorway, their eyes round and accusing.

"We didn't get to hang up our stockings for Santa Claus," Richie said.

"Oh, Moggy forgot," Margaret said. "We'll do it now."

"Where's Mommy?" said Richie, his voice rising in alarm. "Where's my Mommy? I want my Mommy!"

"Want my Mommy!" Davy echoed, and began to cry.

"Mommy and Daddy went to ride in the car," explained Margaret.

"I wanna ride inna car," howled Davy. Richie's face was puckering to follow suit.

"Davy, why don't you be like Richie?" Margaret said quickly. "Richie's big, and he doesn't cry."

Richie pursed his lips and swaggered a bit. "Don't be a baby, Davy," he said.

But Davy *was* a baby, and Margaret's heart ached for him. If Mother died, Richie and Davy might have to be sent to foster homes and have a lot of other mothers.

"Come to sister," she said, and Davy wept in her arms. She let him cry a few minutes, then tickled him until they were all laughing. They hung their stockings and Margaret got them back into bed, Richie boasting loudly about what Santa would bring them, and Davy heavy-eyed for sleep.

Then she got out the box of ornaments and trimmed the tree just like last year. When she was through it looked simply beautiful, with bright balls and silver icicles. The Christmas angel on top tipped only a little.

Last of all, she filled stockings for the boys and one for Mother and Daddy, except theirs were so big that everything she could find, even with the orange, filled only the toes. It didn't seem enough, so she got her four quarters from the last allowance money and put one in each stocking. With a last-minute hope, and feeling a little ashamed, she hung one up for herself, but she didn't fill it.

When midnight came, Daddy still hadn't come or called. She opened the door to look out. The snow was coming down in great flakes, blurring the outlines of the gate, making a dim, yellow blob of the street light and muffling the last strains of "Silent Night" from some-where down the street.

Margaret closed the door and went to sit on the couch and wait for Daddy. The next thing she knew it was morning. Richie and Davy were up, exploring their stockings with shrieks of delight. It took a dazed moment for Margaret to get her bearings. Daddy was still not home, and alarm beat up in her chest.

"See, I've got nuts and real chocolates and a money," Richie exulted. Margaret's eyes went to her stocking in spite of herself. Of course it was hanging limp and empty beside Mother's and Daddy's, as she knew it would be, but she couldn't keep from hoping.

"Eat your oranges before you have candy," she told the boys.

She helped them untie the knots of the packages, showed them how to wind up their toys and build hills of the rugs for the jeep and tractor to climb before the telephone finally rang. It was Daddy, his voice thin and high.

"I'm coming home soon, Margaret, but I have news for you. Don't tell the boys, because I want to surprise them. We have a new baby sister."

Margaret leaned her head against the wall.

"Are you there, Margaret?"

"Yes, Daddy. Is—is Mother living?"

"Yes, Molly. What made you ask?"

It was all Margaret could do to keep from crying. "I thought she would die. I was afraid."

"Just between you and me, Molly, I thought so too, and I was afraid, but she's all right now. The doctor says she will be just fine. Just be a good girl until I get home, and that's all I'll want of you. The lady Mother arranged for is coming to help us."

Blindly, Margaret hung up the telephone. Daddy had said so himself—he wouldn't need her anymore. Besides, there was her promise. The Lord had kept His part.

She went to her room to pack, the dear little room with the pink roses and the dressing table Daddy had made for her. The pretty dresses Mother had made filled her suitcase real tight because of their fullness. She had to pack her treasures in a paper sack. There was the blue horse with the spangled mane Richie gave her for her birthday, two Christmas dolls, and the pink satin ribbon she was saving for a special occasion.

When she came out with her hat and coat on, the suitcase banging against her leg, Daddy was there, Richie and Davy clambering all over him. "I want my baby sister now," Richie demanded.

When Daddy saw Margaret, his face sobered. "What's this, Margaret! What are you doing with your suitcase?"

"I'm ready to go back to Miss Billings now, to find me a new home."

"For Pete's sake," said Daddy. He backed to a chair, still looking at her, and sat down. "Come here, Margaret," he said.

Margaret came slowly and he pulled her onto his knee.

"What did you get for Christmas?"

Margaret didn't answer, because she would cry if she did.

"Nothing," Daddy said. "I can see your stocking, and it is empty. Is that why you want to go?"

"No, Daddy," said Margaret, ashamed that he would think her that babyish.

"Then why are you going?"

"The baby's a girl, and you won't want to keep me.

She will fill Mother's need for a daughter," she said, carefully repeating the words Daddy had said. "And Mother won't have so many to wash and cook for."

"Where'd you get that idea? Who told you that?"

"You said it, and I heard. I didn't mean to listen."

"When did I say a thing like that?" Daddy didn't sound believing.

"Last summer. And Mother said if the baby was a girl—"

All the breath went out of Daddy. "Molly. Molly," he said sadly. "Now I remember. And all the time you've been carrying around these thoughts?"

Margaret's voice wouldn't go past the ache in her throat. Her eyes smarted, and her nose felt thick and runny.

"Listen, Molly. We need you now more than ever. Last night, when Mother was so sick, she kept saying, 'Thank goodness for Margaret!' And you know what she said when the doctor told her it was a girl? She said, 'Now we're even. Two boys and two girls.'"

"Oh, Daddy!" said Margaret, her heart full.

"She told me where she hid your gift—in her bottom dresser drawer—she sewed a pink silk dress to go with your satin ribbon. Now I'll tell you my gift," he said, shifting her to get his handkerchief and blow his nose. "Your mother and I have been talking to the judge of the Juvenile Court, and at last we are sure we can adopt you."

Margaret couldn't hold back the sobs any longer. They came hard and deep with relief. Daddy just held her tighter and patted her and said, "There now, cry if you want to, little Molly."

Finally she was quiet and peaceful. Suddenly, she thought of something.

"I didn't fill a stocking for the baby!" She slipped off his lap and ran to get a tiny stocking from the layette.

"It's pink for girls, isn't it, Daddy?" she asked, putting her pink satin ribbon in it. But he was asleep in the chair.

Margaret shushed Davy and Richie and took them from the room. Then she brought an afghan and tucked it tenderly about her father.

"Merry Christmas, Daddy," she whispered. "This is the best Christmas ever."

About the Author

Alice Morrey Bailey, at age 93, is a veteran author and poet who still makes a daily habit of writing. She is a frequent contestant in all literary genres, and has won writing awards since 1940, 1,050 awards since 1976 alone. She is also a sculptor whose work is on permanent display in eight museums, and the composer of several award-winning piano pieces.

Alice, who has been a widow for twenty-four years, has three children, fourteen grandchildren, 50 great-grandchildren, and seven great-great-grandchildren. She is a lifelong member of The Church of Jesus Christ of Latter-day Saints, and has held many positions in the auxiliary organizations.

Alice is a resident of Salt Lake City, Utah.

THE LAST GIFT
OF CHRISTMAS

BY JOAN LISONBEE SOWARDS

I

Cynthia Charles sped the red compact over the Vermont countryside, enjoying its beauty. The barren trees reached trunk and limb through a blanket of snow towards the morning sun, peeking its soft rays through heavy clouds that threatened snow. It was cold outside, but the car heater kept the small compartment comfortable. This country was new to her. In spite of the snow all around, the roads were clear of any ice. She gripped the steering wheel of the small rental car even tighter as it rounded a sharp curve. Suddenly, the beautiful scene of a small Vermont village lay before her. She slowed as she passed through the town.

Cynthia, her husband Rick, and his partner, Todd Andersen, had flown into Albany the night before. Rick and Todd planned to sign a contract with a growing corporation in Albany, J.R. Pelling Co. Cynthia had taken the opportunity to come along with Rick, leaving their three teenagers in the care of the oldest, who was home from college on Christmas break.

Christmas was three days past. Cynthia felt relieved

now that it was over. She hoped this trip would allow her and Rick to spend some needed time together.

She loved Rick, she was sure of that, but they seemed to have drifted apart in the last few years. Their twenty-two years of marriage had been happy, but now Rick was so involved in his successful computer software company that they hardly saw each another. She enjoyed being with their children, going to their ball games and concerts, yet her heart often ached with loneliness for Rick.

His partner, Todd, was single and spent as much time with the business as Rick did. Sometimes she sensed that Rick was a bit envious of Todd's not having the added responsibility of a family.

Evidence that Christmas had come to Vermont was everywhere. Homes and trees were laced with lights and garland. Cynthia thought of her own Christmas, and a sadness came over her as she remembered the sweater Rick had given her. It was beautiful and undoubtedly expensive. Convinced that he had given it as a formality, an obligation with no thought put into it, she had resisted the temptation of asking who had picked it out. She imagined him giving one of the office girls his credit card and asking her to pick up a gift for his wife—the most beautiful thing she could find.

They had eaten dinner in the hotel's elegant restaurant soon after their arrival. Rick's thoughts were still on work and his presentation for the next day, and he seemed distant from her as they returned to their room and dressed for bed. He was already in the early stages of snoring as she crawled into bed beside him and laid her head on his chest.

"I love you, Rick," she whispered.

"I love you, too," he said between sputters of a snore. Then he was off to sleep.

Suddenly, Cynthia was startled out of her daydream as she came around a bend in the road, almost hitting a white-tailed deer. Screaming, she swerved to miss the animal, running her car off the road and bouncing over thirty feet of snow-covered rocks. The engine stopped and the young deer trotted quietly away, unaware of the trauma it had caused.

Cynthia began to sob. "This isn't my car!" she screamed through her tears as she fumbled for the door handle. Unable to open the door in her panic, she turned the ignition key for power and rolled down the window. She pulled herself up and sat on the window ledge, wiped her tears, and surveyed the situation. What was she going to do?

Remembering the dress boots she had thrown in the rear seat, she crawled back into the car. She slipped her street shoes off, pulled on the boots, then lifted herself out and onto the ground.

It was cold! She was glad she had worn wool pants. The thermometer in the car read twenty degrees. She reached back in to pull out a black hooded parka and slipped it on as she tried to walk around the car, looking for damages. With each step, her boots slipped on the rocks and ice. The front of the car was lodged on a large boulder, and the fiberglass fenders were well scratched. She unsuccessfully tried the door handle again, gave up, and crawled back through the window. She turned the key, hoping the car would start. It did, but the tires spun in the rocks and snow.

"Now what am I going to do?" she cried. She debated whether she should start walking or wait for help. It was too cold to walk, she determined as she rolled up the window. The road map she had been using was crumpled from her attempts to crawl in and out of the car. She picked it up and examined it. Chatterleigh was her destination; she finally found the road on the map. It turned off the main highway about two miles down the road. From there, it was one mile to the town.

She attempted to open the door again. Aha! It had to be unlocked first. In her fluster, she hadn't figured on that. The door opened easily, but because of the angle, it barely opened far enough for her to squeeze through. Slipping her camera into her purse and locking the car, she carefully made her way over the rocks and back to the road.

It seemed strange that there was no traffic. Cynthia had been there at least fifteen minutes, and not one car had come by. It was so cold—*too cold to be out walking,* she thought, pulling the hood over her head and securing it under her chin.

Chatterleigh . . . her great-great-grandparents had lived and were buried there. Before boarding the plane, she had promised her grandmother that she would take pictures of the place.

She looked up the road toward Chatterleigh. *Three miles isn't too far to walk,* she thought. Surely someone would be coming by and could give her a lift.

Keeping up a steady pace, she had traveled a long

way before she heard a vehicle approaching. She had never hitched a ride before and felt afraid. She turned, out of breath, at the side of the road and regretfully watched a truck pass by and disappear over the hill. In the mud clinging to the back of the truck was scribbled, "Merry Christmas."

Yes, *Christmas,* she thought, and the sad twinge returned. She had spent weeks worrying about her present for Rick. He loved computers, and . . . well, there wasn't much else he did anymore. Most of his time was spent with his software company. He did very well, and had provided abundantly for her and the children. *Why aren't you happy, then?* she kept asking herself. She *was* proud of him for his accomplishments, but it seemed to have come in exchange for the closeness they had once shared.

After searching in vain for the perfect gift, she had finally bought him new clothes and a subscription to *Business Times and Computers.* She couldn't go wrong with either choice, because he depended on her to keep him dressed and he read *BT&C* as if it were the Bible. He thanked her graciously for the gifts, but she suspected that he probably thought the same of her gift as she did his: that she hadn't put much thought into it.

Finally, Cynthia reached the turn to Chatterleigh. It was reassuring to see a sign pointing the way. The steeple of a church peeked over the hill. It looked like a welcome sign waiting just for her. The bells in the steeple chimed twelve o'clock and then began playing "Joy to the World." Feeling a new surge of energy, she picked up her pace. The beautiful music was accompanied by the wind whistling through the trees.

At the top of the hill, she stopped abruptly. The scene below was breathtaking. In the center of the village proudly stood a glowing white church with its towering steeple. Snow covered the lawns of the neatly kept homes. The whole scene was beautiful, as if on a postcard.

As Cynthia stood appreciating the view, it began to snow. *Just my luck,* she thought as she started down the hill. *How can I take pictures or walk through graveyards when it's snowing? Well, Grandma, I've kept my word. I'm here at Chatterleigh.*

II

The town seemed deserted. Cynthia headed straight for the church, seeing a cemetery in its yard. The snow fell faster, and it was hard to see. She buried her hands deeper into the pockets of the parka and kept her head down in an attempt to keep the snow out of her face. Arriving at the church, she climbed the stairs, reluctantly withdrawing her hand from the warm pocket to hold tightly to the cold wrought iron handrail. Once under the shelter of the porch, she tried to brush herself free of snow, her hands stinging from the cold.

Shoving her hands back into her pockets, she leaned against one of the double doors. To her surprise, the door opened. Slowly, she pushed the entrance wider and stepped into the foyer of the chapel, quietly closing the door behind her.

Cynthia hadn't been in a church for many years. It felt strange, but peaceful. The foyer ran the full width of the chapel and had a dropped ceiling. She wondered if the ceiling was the floor of an organ loft. Oh yes, there were the stairs to the far left. A silence, no, a reverence filled the air of the dimly lit chapel. She thought back to the days when she and Rick had gone to church every Sunday. Through the years, other things had taken its place. Rick became so busy with his company, and she didn't like taking the children alone, and . . . well, the usual excuses.

To her right stood a tall, decorated fir tree, and to her left, a few feet away, was a cast iron stove giving off a most welcome heat. She tiptoed over to it, trying not to make a sound that might interrupt the reverence. It felt so good to have heat after that long, cold hike from the mountain.

Her feet longed to be free of the dress boots. She looked around for a chair, but there wasn't one. Several rows of pews faced a simple pulpit and a large wooden cross on the wall at the front of the room. A Christmas star stood about three feet tall in front of the pulpit. There was an aisle that divided the pews down the middle, and one aisle on each side along the walls. White, lightweight curtains covered three tall, Gothic windows at each side of the room.

Cynthia removed the heavy parka and looked for a place to hang it. To the far left of the foyer was a coat cove, with many hooks on its inner wall. She tiptoed over to the cove and found a wooden bench in the darkness on which to sit and remove the boots. She managed to remove the first one before she heard a door open and slow, shuffling footsteps enter the chapel. She stopped and held her breath. Of course, whoever it was didn't know that she was in the cove. She wondered what she should do; it would look as though she were trying to hide if she stayed there. She gathered her courage and stood, boot in hand, and stepped out of the shadows.

The footsteps belonged to an old man with white hair, wearing a plaid shirt under a pair of worn overalls. He slowly approached, slightly hunched as he walked down the aisle on the other side of the room. He hadn't looked up to see her. She called hello, but still he didn't stop. He must not have heard her. She called again, but he still didn't look up. Now she felt determined, and walked over to the end of the aisle. That's when he saw her and smiled, revealing a mouth full of worn, stained teeth.

"Hello, young lady," he said with surprise. Reaching in his pocket, he retrieved a small object. "Let me put my hearing aid in, and then I can hear what you say . . . now, what can I do for you?"

"I got caught in the snow. I hope it's all right that I came in," she answered, motioning to the door with boot in hand.

"Sure it's all right. You're welcome here," the old man assured her. "Wouldn't be much of a church if it couldn't shelter a cold traveler. You from these parts?" he asked, knowing perfectly well she wasn't.

"My car is a few miles south of town. I had a little accident trying to miss a deer on the road. The car is stuck in a pile of rocks." She tried to be brief, still holding the boot. "Are you the reverend here?"

"No, no, just the caretaker. Did you catch a ride into

town?" the old man queried as he resumed his journey to the back of the room.

"No, I walked." Cynthia replied, remembering the only truck that had passed her on the road.

"While it was snowing? And it's so cold out there!" The old man stopped and turned, waiting to hear her answer.

"No, it only started snowing when I was at the top of the hill."

"Are you putting on that shoe or taking it off?" he asked, shaking a gnarled finger at the boot.

She looked at it and laughed. "Oh, I was taking it off. I wanted to warm my cold feet by your stove . . . if that's okay."

"Be my guest," he said, walking over to the stove and opening the door. "I'll bring a few more logs for the fire and a chair so you can make yourself comfortable. He shuffled from the room through a door opposite the coat cove while she went over to the stove and warmed her hands. He returned a few minutes later with a small brown chair and a log nestled under his arm. "Here you go," he said, quite out of breath. "Sit right here and warm your feet."

Cynthia sat on the straight-back chair and removed the second boot. Her feet wanted to be free of the socks, too, so off they came. She got as comfortable as she could while the old gentleman continued shuffling around the chapel.

He began to talk from across the room. "What are you planning to do about your car? Our town mechanic has gone over to Barre for the holidays to be with his daughter. His tow truck is still here, but he's the only one who has ever operated it."

"I guess I'll try to call my husband, but I probably won't be able to reach him right now. He'll be in meetings with a client in Albany, probably until five or six o'clock."

"We could call a tow truck up from Rutland, but I can't imagine anyone wanting to go out into snow like this," the old man mused. "You're welcome to stay here in our church house until you can get some help. Use the phone, too, if you'd like."

She turned to him. "Thank you, that is very generous of you."

"Well, if you are going to be sticking around here for a while, we might as well get acquainted. I'm Harold," the old man said.

"I'm Cynthia," she replied. "Glad to meet you."

The wind picked up and whistled through the old structure. "Ah, that's nothing," Harold said. "This old church has been through many a blizzard in its day. Why, when the Woodburys' roof fell in from the weight of the snow, they all stayed here and slept on these pews 'til the roof was fixed. They had seven kids, and those kids were a blizzard! If this place could survive all those rowdy kids, it can survive anything." He added, shaking his head, "All those kids are grown and married now."

Cynthia turned and looked over the quiet chapel. She could imagine little children playing tag among the pews. She smiled, remembering her own children when they were young. There could be many people sleeping now, unseen on the pews, and she would never know because the pews had their backs to her. All this made her aware of how tired she was. Sleeping on a pew didn't sound so bad to her right now.

Harold must have read her thoughts. "I know where there's a blanket and pillow. They were collected for the needy family Christmas drive, and nobody seemed to need them. But here you are, and you need them, so I guess they were meant for you." With that he shuffled back out of the room.

Cynthia waited quietly on her chair, still warming her feet by the stove. After a few minutes she stood and padded barefoot to the nearest window. Drawing back the thin, white curtain, she peered out. The cemetery didn't look like much more than a blur of white through the falling snow. The images of headstones in the yard reminded her of the task that had brought her here.

The old gentleman returned to the chapel with the bedding. "You'll probably be wanting an afternoon nap before long," he said. "You must be tired from all that walking. The snow is coming so fast that I don't see how you will get out of here before the day's over." He dropped the blanket and pillow on the nearest pew.

"I was planning to explore the cemetery to find my family's graves today, but it doesn't look like I'm going to get a chance," she sighed.

"Oh, who is your family?" the old man asked, sliding his hands deep into his pockets.

"The name is Weatherby. They are supposed to be buried somewhere in Chatterleigh." She returned to the heat of the cast iron stove.

"They are right here by this wall." He pointed to

where she had just peeked out. "There's no Weatherbys living in Chatterleigh anymore. The young ones all grew up and left, and the old ones died off."

"My great-grandmother was one of those young ones, I guess," Cynthia replied. "I'd better call and leave a message at the hotel for my husband so he will know where I am. May I use the phone now?"

"You bet," he said and turned, expecting her to follow.

At that moment the chapel doors burst open, and a figure entered wearing a lady's overcoat, knee-high galoshes, and carrying an umbrella.

"Stella! What are you doing out in this blizzard?" The old man stopped in his tracks.

"The phones are all out!" said the woman, turning to shake the snow from the umbrella. "I came over to tell you and bring your lunch." She closed the door and slipped off the galoshes. She was an older woman with white hair, her face full of wrinkles. Her blue eyes danced with excitement as she panted from her hurried trip. She drew a large brown paper sack from under her overcoat and set it on the floor. Then she took off the heavy coat.

"All the phones are out?" The old man resumed his journey, fumbling with a large ring of keys hanging from his belt loop. After selecting one, he stopped at a closed door and unlocked it. He disappeared into the dark room, and after a few moments returned. "You're right. Dead. Dead as a doorpost," he confirmed. "Stella, this is Cynthia. Her car is stranded a few miles out of town." Then he turned to Cynthia. "Stella is my bride of fifty-eight years."

"Wow, that's great!" Cynthia replied. "I can't imagine being married so long."

"It's been a happy life for us," Harold added. "Stella, I figure Cynthia is pretty hungry, too. She has walked a long way this morning."

"I have enough food here for everyone," the older woman said cheerfully as she settled down on a pew and brought out roast beef sandwiches, carrot sticks, milk, and two cups from the sack. "I was thinking I would stop by and check on a few elderly neighbors and make sure they were safe, and brought along extra sandwiches for some of them. Harold, would you run to the kitchen and get a glass for this young lady to use? Bring a knife, too."

Harold obediently hobbled off, and Cynthia turned to Stella. "How am I going to get word to my husband? I really need to let him know where I am." She sat down near Stella.

"As soon as the storm is over, they'll get to work on the phone lines and you'll be able to call him," Stella assured her.

"Does anyone in your town have a cellular phone?"

"No, we're just old folks living close to the church here," the old woman said. "We don't own anything fancy like that. Do you like roast beef?"

"Yes, thank you so much."

Stella continued talking as she served Cynthia. "You see, the children grow up and go off to college. Most of them never come back here to live. Those who do stay move out to the farms. That leaves just us old folks here in town. The young 'uns love to come back to visit on holidays, though. We have some wonderful reunions, especially at Christmastime . . . I trust you had a merry Christmas?"

"Oh yes, I did, thank you," Cynthia answered, and the twinge of pain returned. How would Rick react to her being snowed in here? Considering the way their relationship had gone lately, she really didn't know.

Harold returned with the glass and the knife. Stella poured the milk. There was plenty of food for all.

"When was this church house built?" Cynthia asked before biting into her sandwich.

"I don't remember the year," the old man began, looking to his wife for the answer. She shook her head and he continued. "It was about the turn of the century. Those were the good old days. We had lots of families and children here in Chatterleigh. When I was just a boy, I climbed the bell tower every Sunday and rang the chimes. What a thrill it was! I'd ring them on Christmas, too. Oh, how I wish I were young again; I'd go right up there and ring them for you. The chimes are on an automatic timer now, and it just doesn't seem the same." He went on and on about different ministers who had served there, and reminisced about many residents of the town.

The three had finished eating, and everything was put back into the sack. Cynthia, feeling a bit chilly, had wrapped the blanket around her and listened with great interest to Harold's stories. When he finished she said, "It is a lovely chapel, and the chimes are beautiful. I heard them on my way down the hill into town."

The old woman took a turn at storytelling. "Even though we are mostly old folk around here, we still take care of one another. We always have. It's a close-knit community. We love our chapel and have taken good care of it. I remember way back, during the war, when so many of our husbands and sons were away. Here it was, Christmas and all, and we were sitting around feeling sorry for ourselves. Someone suggested we make a beautiful star and hang it from the ceiling of the chapel. So, we did. We must have put five pounds of glitter on it," she laughed. "I half expected it to fall, but it didn't. Glistening so brightly up there, it really lifted our spirits."

"Is that the same star, there at the front of the chapel?" Cynthia asked, nodding toward the pulpit.

"Yes," Stella sighed. "It has lost most of its glitter, but we still drag it out of the storeroom every December. It makes us feel good and stands as a reminder of sacrifice. We each sacrificed for our country, and Jesus was born to sacrifice for us."

Cynthia sat quietly thinking. A star that stood for sacrifice. It had been a long time since she had thought about true sacrifice.

Harold interrupted her thoughts. "Old Mrs. Oaks complained every year that we needed a nativity scene. The reverend, for some reason, shuddered whenever she said it. Without fail, each November at the monthly church planning meeting she would stand there at the front of the chapel and say emphatically, 'We can put it right here,' and stamp her foot. I can still hear her high, squeaky voice . . . and finally, we did. It was live—I mean, real people: Mary, Joseph . . . a sheep came, too, until we decided it smelled too bad. And baby Jesus was old Mrs. Oaks' grandson. She sat right on the front row and cried. The tears were streaming down her face. I'll never forget it. We made her very happy that year." He paused for a moment, then added, "She died the next spring. Went back to her Maker."

The three sat in silence for a few minutes, touched by the story and listening to the wind.

The old man stood. "Cynthia, why don't you lie down and get some rest? The snow has lightened up, and Stella and I will go check on the neighbors. You'll have the place to yourself. I'm sure you'll be fine here," Harold assured her. They put on coats and boots, and soon were on their way out the door.

Cynthia stretched out on a pew with her pillow and blanket and tried to relax. In her mind, she rehearsed the accident again. Her terrified feelings returned as she remembered running off the road and bumping over the rocks. She had to get word to Rick somehow. Would he worry about her? Maybe he would go to dinner with his clients, and not even notice that she was still gone until late tonight. Would he even remember where she said she was going? So many questions milled around in her tired mind.

The pain returned and she began to cry. She sat up. "Oh, I don't like crying lying down," she whined to herself, and began looking for a tissue in her purse. The cross on the front wall caught her eye. It had been many years since she had turned to God for help in her life. "Please, Father, help me get out of this mess. Help me get word to Rick. And help Rick not to worry."

A tissue found, she dried her tears, laid her head back down on the pillow, and closed her eyes. In her mind, she thought she saw Christ with his hand stretched out to her. "Be at peace," He told her. "With faith, nothing is impossible."

"I'll have faith. And tell Rick I love him," she whispered as she relaxed and drifted off to sleep.

III

Richard Charles looked down at the note in his hand. He had heard what his client was saying, but he was trying to understand what the words on the paper meant.

"This software package will put us head and shoulders above our closest competitor. Rick, do you hear what I'm saying? I'm saying you two are geniuses," the man emphasized.

Rick crumpled the paper in his hand. "I hear what you're saying and appreciate your compliment, but something has come up and I need to make a quick phone call. I'll try to hurry." He rose from the conference table where his partner and several other men and women were seated and quickly left room. "Where are the phones?" he demanded at the front desk. A young woman directed him down a hall, and he quickly dialed the number on the crumpled paper.

"Hello," he said with urgency in his voice. "This is Rick Charles. I received a message about my rental car being found in Vermont."

"Yes, Mr. Charles. Thank you for calling," was the

response from the young man on the other end of the line. "The Vermont Highway Patrol just notified us that the car you rented was found on Highway 7 in the Green Mountains above Rutland. It appeared to have been in an accident. Do you know anything about this?"

"No, this is the first I've heard of it. Where is my wife? Is she okay?" Rick inquired.

"There was no one with the car when it was found. A search was made of the immediate area, but the blizzard made any more than that impossible. They've even had to close the area."

"Blizzard?" He turned toward the windows, which were framing a beautiful snowfall. This was the first that he had been aware of any snow.

"Surely she is all right, sir," the young man assured him. "There are farmhouses all along that road. Most likely someone gave her a lift, or she walked to shelter."

"Let's hope she's safe. Did the highway patrol leave a number?" he questioned, reaching for a pen.

"Yes sir, just a minute." The young man put him on hold for what seemed longer than necessary. "Here it is, sir," the young man said hurriedly. He quoted the number, and Rick hung up before any good-bye was said.

A deep voice answered at the highway patrol.

"Could you help me, please? My rental car was found on Highway 7, and my wife was driving it. I need to know any information you have about it," Rick said, stumbling over his words.

"Can you hold please?" was the answer, and he heard an immediate click. *Oh, please don't leave me waiting,* Rick thought. He felt frustrated. He knew the meeting was waiting on him. Finally, the deep voice returned. "We have no more information. Who did you say was driving the car?"

"My wife, Cynthia Charles. She's got to be out there somewhere. We've got to find her!"

"Sir, there is a blizzard covering the state. The road has been closed to travel of any type."

Rick gave the man the hotel's phone number and pleaded with him to call as soon as any new information was known. He went back to the front desk. "Have there been any messages for me? Richard Charles, Room 361."

"No, sir," the young woman answered after checking her computer.

Disappointed and confused, Rick stopped at a large picture window and looked out on the falling snow. This business deal with J.R. Pelling was important to him, but how could he just sit here when Cynthia was out there somewhere in all that snow? He had never been good at showing it, but he loved her. She meant so much more to him than any contract. But he knew if he left now to find her, they might lose the deal completely.

The group in the conference room had decided to take a break in Rick's absence. Todd and a few others had returned to the room.

"Rick, what's wrong? Your face is white," Todd exclaimed.

"Cynthia had an accident in Vermont, and they can't find her. Apparently she's lost somewhere in this blizzard," he reported.

"What are they doing to locate her?" another man

asked.

"Nothing. The blizzard is preventing any kind of search. I can't just wait here. I've got to go look for her."

"Rick, that's ludicrous, especially if there's a blizzard. Anyway, you have a presentation to make at four o'clock. You can't leave now. Why don't you wait until this evening? Maybe you'll hear from her by then." Todd was concerned, but practical.

"I wouldn't be able to concentrate enough to make the presentation. Anyway, you could do it just as well as I could," Rick assured him as he gathered his things together.

"I'm no speaker! You've always been the spokesman of this outfit!" Todd protested.

"You'll have to do it," Rick said, taking a firm grip on Todd's arm.

"Mr. Charles, the CEO of our company will be here at ten in the morning to close the deal," a woman pointed out. "You have to be present to sign the papers. Mr. Andersen is right. Why don't you wait until this evening? Maybe you'll hear from your wife by then."

Rick shook his head. "Call your CEO and postpone it, or take Todd's signature as good. I've got to go. I have no choice." With that, he left the room.

IV

The drive to Vermont couldn't go fast enough for Rick. The rental company provided a four-wheel-drive truck for the trip. They claimed the machine would go through anything. Rick had never operated anything so big.

As he drove, he tried to recall what Cynthia had told him before she left that morning. It was something about Vermont and cemeteries and her grandmother. But what? He had been so worried about his own business of the day, the meeting and presentation, getting the contract and all, that he hadn't really listened to her. He felt guilty now that he hadn't taken time to check the weather forecast before she left. He would have done it for himself if he had been the one traveling.

Thoughts of Cynthia filled his mind as he drove on. How beautiful she looked as she knelt at the altar the day they were married. How much love he felt for her as she gave birth to each of their children. She nearly starved with him while he struggled to get their software business going. They had shared so much of life together that he couldn't bear the thought of losing her.

He finally crossed the New York/Vermont border. Because of the snow, it took much more than an hour to make the forty-mile trip to Rutland. Following the road signs, he found Highway 7. He ignored the warning signs announcing the highway closure at Pittsford. He had to stop many times to clear his windshield wipers of new snow.

When he reached the roadblock he slowed and looked around, but saw no one. He carefully rounded the barricade and went on his way. It wasn't easy for him to drive in snow; he wasn't used to such weather, and had only ventured out on roads that snowplows had already cleared. At a crucial turn, he was driving too fast and almost lost control of the vehicle. Fear overtook him for a moment. He knew that if anything happened to him, it would be a long time before anyone would be able to help.

"Oh God," Rick prayed aloud. "It's been a long time since I've prayed, and I'm sorry. I've got to make it up this road, and I've got to find Cindy. I can't lose her, God. I just couldn't live without her. You know that. Please, help me get to her—and please keep her safe. I promise I'll never forget you again. I promise." Tears flowed freely down his cheeks. "Quit crying like a baby, Rick," he scolded himself and wiped his face.

Slowly the truck crept along. It was a continual struggle to stay on the highway. The road seemed to go on forever. The snowfall became heavier, and he couldn't see the road anymore—just an image of a path through the hills and trees in front of him. He tried to stay in the center of that path.

After what seemed like hours, he came to the form of a car covered with snow. Pulling on his parka, he climbed out of the truck and waded through knee-deep snow over to the form. With a bare hand, he brushed the snow from the roof. The car was bright red. He was positive it was his rental. He cleared the window to assure himself that Cynthia wasn't inside.

He crawled back into the truck and sounded the horn several times, just in case . . . in case she could hear it. Then he slowly drove on up the hill. No homes were in sight. Where were all the farmhouses the young man at the car rental agency had talked about? Were they under all this snow?

Finally, he came to a road sign. He got out of the truck and waded over to it. His hands stung before he had cleared the snow enough to read what it said: *CHATTERLEIGH, 1 mile.* The arrow pointed to the right. The hillside was clear of trees, and Rick could not see any image of a road. Something told him that Chatterleigh was where he needed to go. It sounded so familiar. Was this the place Cynthia had told him she was going? How was he to get there if he couldn't find the road?

A branch, barely hanging by its last fiber from a tree that stood beside him, caught his eye. Rick waded over and freed it. Then, using it as a shovel, he found the asphalt road and determined its direction. He drove the truck a few feet, then got out and searched for the asphalt again. This process was taking too long. The sun was setting fast. "Dear God! I need your help! I can't do it by myself," he pleaded again. "Help me find the road."

Then words came to his mind. "Be at peace. With faith, anything is possible. Have faith in me, and I will lead you."

Have faith? he wondered. What other choice did he have at this point? He started the truck slowly toward the top of the steep hill. The tires spun, then caught, and the truck moved forward, then the tires spun again. Through this process he made it to the top of the hill.

The lights of the village below sparkled through the falling snow. They were a welcome sight and gave him new hope. With the sunlight quickly dissipating, it was too dark to attempt taking the truck down the hill. He gathered his belongings and headed out on foot, feeling a sense of urgency. Stumbling many times, he would get back on his feet and continue. Bruised and exhausted, he finally reached the village.

The lights of the church house seemed to beckon him. If there were people there, maybe one of them had seen Cynthia. There was soft organ music playing as he quietly opened the door. The chapel looked empty except for Harold, who was lifting logs into the cast iron stove.

"Hello," Rick called breathlessly, closing the door. "I'm looking for my wife. Her car is stranded on the highway over the hill, and I think she was coming here today. I've got to find her. Can you help me?"

Cynthia, who had been sleeping on a pew, was awakened by the voices. She opened her eyes. It took a few moments for her to remember where she was. Stella stopped playing the organ in the loft to listen to what the men were saying.

"Yes, a young lady came here today. She said her name was Cynthia," Harold answered in a whisper.

"Hurray!" shouted Rick. "Where is she?"

"Now, keep your voice down. She's asleep. Walked all the way from her car this morning, and she's pretty well exhausted."

"Oh, just let me see her so I'll know she's all right. I won't wake her," Rick pleaded, trying to whisper.

"Leave your wet coat over there on the rack and follow me," Harold instructed.

Cynthia smiled and nestled into her pillow. This was the first concern Rick had shown for her in months, and it surprised her. She smiled, nestled into her pillow, and waited to see what would happen next.

After the coat was hung up, the two men quietly

came down the aisle to where she was lying.

"Hello Rick," she said, sitting up.

"Cindy, oh Cindy!" He knelt beside her and took her into his arms. "I was so afraid I had lost you. When the highway patrol said you were in an accident and not with the car, I didn't know what to think."

"Rick, you risked your life by coming here through this storm. What about your meetings?"

"I just couldn't sit by and wait; I just couldn't. I love you too much."

His words melted the last traces of pain in her heart, and she began to cry. He cried, too. She found peace at last in his arms.

V

The deal with J. R. Pelling Company closed a month later than originally planned. Neither company was hurt by the delay. Rick and Cynthia returned home two days late. He became protective of her, and wasn't going to let her out of his sight for a while. Cynthia didn't mind; she loved the attention. She came to realize that she needed to give Rick more attention, too. Their relationship blossomed following that fateful winter day. Rick kept his resolve to remember the Lord and, as a family, they returned to church.

In early spring, Cynthia received a postcard from Stella and Harold. It was a picture of Chatterleigh. A miracle had happened there that changed her and Rick's lives, and she was thankful.

She slipped the postcard into her desk file, where

another card caught her eye. She pulled it out. It was a list of the gifts she had received at Christmas. Smiling, she looked it over, picked up a pen, and at the bottom of the page, added one last gift. It was a gift that sparkled brightly, like the star that the ladies of Chatterleigh had once made. It had been the best gift of all, and she had neglected to add it to her list.

It was Rick's sacrifice and their renewed love.

About the Author

Joan Lisonbee Sowards holds a degree from Arizona State University. She enjoys writing stories and music (many of her songs have been published), genealogy, singing, and family activities.

Joan and her husband, Dennis, live in Mesa, Arizona. They are the parents of five children.

THE EMPTY MANGER
A Christmas Story

BY ANITA STANSFIELD

A light snow swirled like glitter on frequent gusts of wind, finally settling on the pavement like powdered sugar sprinkled over a chocolate cake. Loralee Thompson drove carefully down the long stretch of highway toward home, her final Christmas purchases nestled in the back seat. The first snow of the season was sparse, yet beautiful nevertheless. But to Loralee's dismay, it had not prompted the magic of that Christmas spirit she'd been trying so hard to feel.

Loralee had shopped and decorated, baked and wrapped. She'd hostessed three Christmas parties, distributed baskets of homemade goodies through the neighborhood and beyond. She'd read every Christmas story she could get her hands on, and played Christmas music constantly. But December twenty-third had dawned, and she hadn't yet felt even one of those familiar warm tingles that she *knew* were supposed to be a part of the season.

The snow had lifted her spirits somewhat, and she'd decided a quick trip to town for some last-minute shopping was just the thing to bring those childhood feelings back to her. But as Loralee pulled into the drive of the elegant ranch house she shared with her husband, Mark, a familiar depression squelched any possible blooming of the Christmas spirit. She dreaded going inside— dreaded the emptiness and silence. No matter how hard she tried to convince herself that keeping busy would ease the ache, it simply didn't work. What was Christmas but a harsh reminder that there should be children in the house, spreading noise and delightful havoc? The holidays only reminded her that another year had passed, and it was still just the two of them.

Loralee carried a load of packages into the house and quickly turned on the stereo. She told herself she enjoyed the music—and she did. But in truth, she knew that playing her favorite Christmas CD ridiculously loud was only a futile attempt to drown out the silence of an empty house.

On her way out to the car to get the last bag, Loralee glanced nostalgically toward the old wood nativity scene displayed on the lawn. Mark's grandfather had made and hand-painted the simple set, with an authentic looking manger and life-size baby Jesus. The paint was fading and cracked, but Mary and Joseph glowed with a beauty that warmed Loralee, especially at night, surrounded by the mass of little white lights that Mark always manipulated into the trees the day after Thanksgiving. Baby Jesus was not visible from a distance, nestled snugly in his bed of real straw, but Loralee often walked across the lawn to admire him. He was as worn and faded as the other figures, but if anything could give Loralee a degree of peace as she struggled through the season, it was this rough replica of all that Christmas meant.

At first, Loralee felt certain her eyes were deceiving her. But as she stepped closer to investigate, the manger was blatantly empty. Tears stung her eyes as she glanced quickly around, perhaps hoping to catch the culprit red-handed. She combed the area, wondering if those mischievous Jenkins boys had just moved it. But a lengthy search still produced no baby Jesus.

"Who would do such a thing?" she snarled at the wind, and got nothing but an extra cold bite at her face in return. Convinced that she was getting all upset over nothing, Loralee tried to come up with a logical explanation. She found Mark hard at work in the barn.

"Lora," he grinned, then paused to kiss her as she approached. "I always welcome such interruptions. But I thought you'd be busy with the Christmas—"

"Oh, there's not that much to do," she insisted.

"Are you all right?" He looked carefully into her eyes.

"Mark, did you take the baby Jesus for any reason? I mean . . . I couldn't imagine why you would, but—"

"Why?" His voice deepened with concern. "What's happened?"

"Well . . . it's gone . . . and . . ." Loralee bit her trembling lip, wondering why she should get upset over such a thing. As always, Mark soothed her emotion and listened with empathy.

"We'll get a new one," he suggested.

"But it won't be the same. Your grandfather made it, and . . ."

"Hey," he touched her chin and wiped a stray tear

from her cheek, "we'll make one, Lora. It'll be all right."

"I'm not sure we can," she retorted a little too sharply. The misgiving in his eyes made her wonder if he'd picked up on the unintended double meaning. Not wanting to concern him, she swallowed hard and tried to smile, then left him to his work and went back to the house.

The moment Loralee walked through the door, she understood why the missing baby Jesus bothered her so much. The empty manger on the lawn seemed little more than a stark reminder of the empty crib standing in the room she hadn't entered for months. When the third opportunity for adoption had fallen through, she simply couldn't bear to think about it any more. So she'd closed the door to the nursery, and a part of her spirit had felt closed ever since.

As long as she could remember, Loralee had wanted children of her own. And what better time of year to enjoy them than at Christmas? She gazed at the picture-perfect tree and wished the ornaments were slightly lop-sided—or maybe even a few on the floor, the result of curious little hands. She eyed the porcelain village, its windows lit up with colored lights and the tiny electric train purring through it, and imagined the fascination of a toddler's eyes to see it come to life. If not for this wretched medical problem of hers, the presents beneath the tree would have been rearranged several times, and most of the bows would be missing. But no. Everything was perfect. There was nothing out of place, not a speck of dirt anywhere. That was the reason Loralee couldn't feel the Christmas spirit, and she knew it. And it was the same reason the missing baby Jesus made her so angry. She started the music over and turned it up louder, then she sat down to cry until the CD ended and the eerie silence settled in again.

The doorbell startled Loralee and she hurried to answer it, quickly checking her face in a mirror on the way.

"Hi!" Janie Swenson grinned broadly and pushed a plate of Christmas cookies into Loralee's hands. "I was just on my way into town with the kids so they could pick out presents for each other, and . . ." She motioned over her shoulder toward the not-so-new mini-van parked in the driveway. It only took a quick glance for Loralee to realize that the five Swenson children were extremely excited and full of energy—all except the baby, whose cries of protest could be plainly heard.

"Well," Janie went on, "I just wanted to drop these by. The things you brought over were so delicious. We had them gone in an hour. You must have baked for a week to come up with all that. I don't know how you do it. Anyway, Frank and the kids loved it, and I even managed to get a little. So, we wanted you to have these cookies. It's not much, but, well . . ." She gave a little giggle. "We had fun. They're not real pretty, but they taste good. You're such good neighbors, and we wanted to wish you a merry Christmas. How are you, anyway?" Janie pushed a hand through her hair and glanced quickly toward the crying baby. The oldest boy was trying to quiet him with some odd toy.

"I'm fine," Loralee lied, glancing down at the haphazardly decorated cookies in her hands. The odd shapes were barely discernible through the gobs of frosting and ridiculously piled candies. "How are *you?* You look tired."

"Oh, me?" Janie giggled again. "I'm always tired. But, well . . . such is life. Thank goodness Christmas is only once a year."

"Amen to that," Loralee said, almost under her breath. While Janie was apparently preparing to say good-bye, Loralee impulsively asked, "Is the baby all right?" As soon as she said it, she wished she hadn't. She hated drawing attention to the fact that she was so naive about babies.

"Oh, he's fine," Janie assured her. "He just hates the car. And his morning nap got cut short because the kids were fighting. I'm sure he'll—"

"Why don't you let me watch him while you go shopping?" Loralee asked, and immediately had the urge to kick herself as she wondered where that had come from. Tending someone else's baby seemed like pouring salt into her open wounds. Had she gone mad?

"Oh," Janie's face showed a combination of relief and hesitance, "I wouldn't want to put you out. I'm sure you have plenty to do yourself for Christmas, and—"

"I have practically nothing to do," Loralee interrupted, setting the cookies aside. Feeling a sudden need to just hold that baby and soothe its cries, she walked toward the car. Janie hurried ahead of her.

Following a flurry of questions and instructions, Loralee found herself standing on the porch with a blanketed bundle and a diaper bag. Janie backed out of the driveway and waved eagerly, but Loralee's hands were full. The baby's apparent relief at being out of the car quickly gave way to fresh wails of protest. Loralee hurried inside to lay him on the couch and unwrap the blankets.

"Hello, Joseph," she said gently as she lifted him to her shoulder. He quieted down, and she turned to get a better look at him as she softly patted his back. A clean baby scent touched her nostrils, and she pressed a quick kiss to the wisp of blond hair. Janie had said he was almost two months old, but he felt so tiny. Were all babies so little?

Loralee lost track of the time as she just held the baby. His tiny eyes seemed to be taking in his surroundings, as if he knew they were unfamiliar, but he felt curious rather than disoriented. She felt proud of herself for successfully changing a diaper, and noticed then that the baby's clothes were clean and smelled fresh. But it was obvious that Joseph was not the first to wear them; more likely the third or fourth. There was evidence of hand mending, and the colors were faded.

When Joseph began to fuss, Loralee fixed a bottle of formula according to Janie's instructions, and sat in the rocker to feed him. He drank the milk eagerly, then Loralee patted his back until he produced an adequate burp. She cradled him against her and offered more milk, but he didn't seem interested. Within a few minutes he was asleep. Again, Loralee felt no sense of time as she cuddled the baby and absorbed his warmth. She realized as she watched him that she felt somehow better. Though she dreaded having to let him go, she was glad she'd offered to watch him. Perhaps, if nothing else, the experience had renewed her confidence in being able to care for a baby.

Mark came in, and the baby jumped slightly in his sleep when the door closed loudly. Loralee heard him shuffling out of his boots and coat, then she looked up to see him watching her. For a long moment he stood motionless; the surprise on his face was evident. She smiled at him and turned her attention back to the sleeping infant.

"You didn't steal it, did you?" he finally asked, a facetious lilt in his voice.

"No," she chuckled softly, "I didn't steal it. This is Janie Swenson's baby. I offered to tend him while she took the other children shopping."

Mark moved slowly closer, as if he felt compelled to ease a childish curiosity. He went down on one knee and kissed Loralee's cheek, but his eyes never left the baby. "He's a cute little thing," he commented. "He's just so . . . *little.*"

"Janie said he's almost two months old," Loralee reported.

"Do you think it would be all right if I hold him?" Mark asked. The intrigue in his voice warmed Loralee, reminding her of the many reasons she loved him.

"Of course," she replied.

"I'll just go wash my hands and warm them up," he said, dashing toward the bathroom. He returned quickly, and Loralee gently placed the sleeping bundle in his arms, where the baby appeared even smaller. Mark chuckled and eased carefully into the rocking chair as Loralee stood. She admired them together for a few minutes, then hurried into the nursery to warm it up and put a clean sheet in the crib. She was already finished before she consciously realized what she'd just done, without feeling any pain at all.

"Do you want to lay him down?" Loralee asked.

"No," Mark replied, "but I suppose I should. I'm starving."

Joseph hardly seemed to notice being shifted to the bed. Loralee tucked a blanket carefully around him, then she watched him quietly while Mark held her tight. They reluctantly went to the kitchen and shared a lunch of leftovers from the previous night's lasagna.

"Are you okay?" Mark asked following a lull of silence.

"Actually, I am," she smiled. "I mean, I admit I don't want to give him up. But it feels good to be helping Janie, and . . . well, he's so sweet."

"That's my girl," Mark smiled and reached over to touch her chin in a familiar gesture of affection. "I see hope in those eyes again."

Loralee's expression sobered. "I hardly dare hope sometimes, Mark. What if—"

"Our day will come," he assured her. "There is *always* hope, Lora. In a way, isn't that what Christmas is all about?"

She thought about it a moment. "Yes, I suppose it is."

Loralee's fledgling hope stayed with her into the afternoon. She was almost disappointed that Joseph slept so well. But she tidied up the house and washed a few dishes, checking on him every few minutes. And she was only slightly dismayed when Janie arrived to pick him up.

"I dropped the kids off at home first," she said as she came through the door. "I had to get five minutes of peace." Janie gave a little laugh. "How was Joseph? Did he—"

"Oh, he was a little angel," Loralee assured her. "He's asleep. Do you want to take him anyway, or . . . would you like to have some hot chocolate with me and—"

"Oh, I'd love to." Janie enthusiastically slipped out of her coat. "It would be wonderful to have someone over twelve to talk to for a change. I mean, Frank's wonderful and all, but he's just so busy all the time, and . . . well, a man's got to make a living."

"Yes, I know about that," Loralee agreed. "Mark's not around nearly enough. It gets kind of lonely, and . . ." She allowed the sentence to fade, as it led to something she didn't want to talk about.

"Do you want to peek at the baby?" Loralee led the way to the nursery without waiting for a response. Janie smiled down at her sleeping son and stroked his wispy head, then she glanced around the room, her eyes widening in surprise. Loralee felt the question on Janie's lips, but she seemed hesitant to verbalize it.

"We're trying to adopt, you see," Loralee explained quickly, "but it's been a long time, and well . . . I thought Joseph might as well make good use of the room while he was here."

For a moment Loralee almost expected Janie to show pity, or perhaps probe her with questions concerning the reason conception was impossible. But Janie only smiled. "I'm sure it will work out with time," she said, as if it were the most natural thing in the world. "Prayers have a way of getting answered eventually, don't they?"

Loralee followed Janie back to the kitchen, feeling a little lighter. She'd gotten in the habit of keeping the problem to herself, as if it might prevent people from hurting her feelings with well-meant advice and questions. But simply sharing it with Janie had already made the problem feel a little less severe.

Janie sat at the table and sampled Christmas goodies while Loralee prepared two cups of mint hot chocolate, and sat down across from her.

"I really appreciate your watching Joseph," she commented. "It's amazing how much faster and easier shopping is without a baby."

"I was glad to do it," Loralee said and meant it.

"I'll return the favor some day," Janie said with a little wink. Loralee just smiled and tried to comprehend such a thing.

"Ah," Janie said as she leaned back and closed her eyes a moment, "it's so good to just sit down for no reason at all. I love Christmas, truly I do. But, oh, it gets hectic at times." Janie glanced around the kitchen. "You really have a lovely home," she commented. "And it's so . . . cozy."

"Really?" Loralee was surprised. She'd always believed it would take children to make her home *cozy*.

"So, what are your plans for Christmas?" Janie asked. "Do you have family close, or—"

"My father lives nearby. My sister and her children live with him. We'll spend much of Christmas Day with them. Mark and I have a nice dinner and such on Christmas Eve."

Janie smiled. "That sounds so . . . peaceful."

"A little too peaceful, perhaps," Loralee replied, wondering what had urged her to be so open with this woman. Was she so starved for friendship?

Loralee wondered for a moment if she might get a probing question about her infertility. But Janie erupted with a gentle little laugh and said, "It seems that you and I have trials at opposite ends of the spectrum." Loralee narrowed her eyes in question, and Janie clarified, "Well, it seems I'm always longing for peace and quiet and a good night's sleep, wondering where all these children came from. And here you've not been blessed with what I have in abundance."

Loralee glanced down briefly, tempted to feel upset. But something in Janie's gentle manner eased her discomfort. "Funny, isn't it?" she replied and took a long sip of her hot chocolate.

"So," Loralee changed the subject, hoping Joseph would continue to sleep, "tell me what the children got for each other. I'm curious."

Janie began a detailed oratory on the drama of contemplation and indecision her children had endured on their shopping excursion. Loralee chuckled at Janie's elaborate gestures as she saw a side to her neighbor she'd never had the chance to see before. She wondered briefly if her seclusion from the neighborhood was her own doing. There were several families in the area that she and Mark were acquainted with, but Loralee had always felt hesitant to be social, perhaps not wanting any more reminders that she was the only childless woman for miles. But Janie Swenson was friendly and open, and by her example encouraged Loralee to be the same.

Loralee kept asking questions about their Christmas celebration, and Janie told her everything the children would be getting. It was easy to see that the Swenson family would have a nice Christmas, but it had been carefully planned and budgeted and would not have extra frills. Janie mentioned that it had been a tighter year than usual, and their Christmas would not be as grand as it had been in years past. But Janie didn't seem to mind. It was obvious she loved her family, and loved sharing this celebration with them—even if she did feel tired and overwhelmed.

Joseph made a squawking cry from the other room and Janie hurried to get him. Loralee expected her to bundle him up and leave, but she sat back down with the baby in her arms as they continued to visit. Loralee was fascinated with the way Janie handled the baby, as if it were as natural as breathing.

"May I hold him?" Loralee asked when he began to seem a little restless. While she cradled the baby, Janie fixed a fresh bottle and handed it to her. "He's seems to be a good baby," Loralee commented, hoping Janie wouldn't realize she had no idea whether he was or not. What little time she'd spent with her sister's children when they were young didn't count for much by way of experience.

"He is good most of the time," Janie answered, "but he certainly likes to play at night. I've not had a full night's sleep since he was born. Well . . ." she chuckled, "it was long before that. Those last few weeks of the pregnancy he played all night, too."

Loralee was intrigued. "How does that feel?" she asked with intense curiosity, realizing she would never experience such a thing.

Janie launched into a fresh bout of conversation about pregnancy and childbirth, sharing details that Loralee would have never imagined. She'd never thought about pregnancy as being miserable, and truthfully had not considered that babies might not sleep at night. It didn't make her want a baby any less, but it did make her stop and think that she had many advantages in her life as it was. Perhaps it would do her some good to make better use of them.

As if Janie had read her mind, she said with natural kindness, "You know, Loralee, I'm certain you'll be able to get a baby one day. But until that happens, just look at all the things you could be doing. What I wouldn't give to just have a free afternoon once in a while!"

"Well," Loralee smiled, "perhaps you and I could help each other out a little. I mean, I've thoroughly enjoyed taking care of Joseph. And Mark did, too. Why don't you let us take the little ones once a week while the older ones are in school?"

"Oh!" Janie leaned back and put a hand to her heart as if she'd just won a sweepstakes. "I don't know what to say. I wasn't hinting or anything by what I said. I just—"

"I know. And I'm telling you it would help me fill up some lonely hours. If what you say is true, and I *do* get the chance for a baby one day, I could use the practice, don't you think?"

"Well," Janie chuckled, "I certainly wouldn't turn down such an offer. We could start after the holidays."

"Great," Loralee said, realizing she felt better in spirit than she had in weeks, possibly months. Was her life so narrow? Was she so accustomed to wallowing in her misery and feeling sorry for herself?

Loralee got a healthy burp out of Joseph just before Janie glanced at her watch and gasped. "Good heavens! I've got so much to do. And who knows what the children have done to the house by now?"

Loralee said little as Janie bundled up the baby and tucked his belongings into the diaper bag. Impulsively she gave Janie a hug at the door, and thanked her for a wonderful afternoon. Their eyes met for a moment, and Loralee wondered if it was just a coincidence that Janie had come into her life today, even if she had lived down the street for years.

Loralee felt a chill of loneliness as she watched Janie drive away. But her warm memories of the time spent with Janie and Joseph melted it away. Idly she straightened up what didn't need straightening, and wandered into the nursery. It looked so empty without Joseph's little round form curled in the center of the crib. But now the emptiness was softened by a new layer of hope. What had Mark said earlier? *There was always hope.* For the first time in months, she almost believed that.

With a fresh zeal, Loralee wrapped the things she'd purchased that morning, then she fixed a meat loaf and scalloped potatoes for supper and put them in the oven. Mark came in right on time. She saw him glance around, a subtle disappointment showing in his eyes.

"Baby's gone, eh?" he asked in a light tone that didn't fool her. She knew he'd enjoyed Joseph as much as she had.

"Yes, but . . ." As Loralee realized what she'd almost said, the idea that had been rolling around in her mind materialized.

"But?" Mark questioned.

"I was thinking . . . what if we give the Swensons a different kind of Christmas gift?"

"And what would that be?" His eyes sparkled with intrigue and amusement.

"A good night's sleep."

"What?" he laughed.

"Janie told me the baby doesn't sleep well, and she hasn't had a good night's sleep since long before he was born. Let's see if they'll let us keep Joseph tonight. What's a night's sleep to us? We can sleep anytime. Everything's ready for Christmas, and . . ." Loralee could hardly speak as she bubbled with excitement.

Mark shook his head in apparent disbelief and chuckled.

"What?" she insisted.

"Do you know how long it's been since I've seen you excited about *anything?*"

"I know," she said, glancing briefly to the floor. "I've been impossibly glum and feeling sorry for myself. It's a wonder you can even put up with me when—"

"Hey," Mark took her shoulders into his hands, "you don't have to apologize or explain. I know how hard it is for you. But one day . . ."

Loralee pulled Mark close and hugged him tightly.

"I love you, Mark. I don't know what I'd ever do without you."

He kissed her warmly, and Loralee had a sudden longing for a romantic evening. But tonight they had other more important matters. Tomorrow evening would be theirs to share alone.

"If it's all right with you," she said eagerly, "I'll call Janie and see if she'll let us take him tonight, and—"

"It's okay with me," he laughed. "I wasn't planning on doing much tomorrow, anyway."

Loralee felt downright nervous when Janie protested her suggestion. "If there is a reason you don't want us to take him," Loralee went on quickly, "or if you're not comfortable with it, I understand. Just be honest with me, and there'll be no hard feelings."

"It's not that," Janie insisted, "it's just that . . . well . . . All night? Are you sure? About three o'clock, you might want to renege on the deal."

"I can assure you, Janie, we have very little to do tomorrow. It would be fun for us to have the baby, and you could get some sleep and get a good start on the things you need to do tomorrow. We'll keep him until late morning or so."

"You're sure?" Janie questioned again.

"Absolutely," Loralee insisted.

"Well," Janie laughed, "I'm certainly not going to turn down a Christmas gift like that! I do believe you're an angel sent from heaven, Loralee."

"I think it's the other way around," Loralee replied.

Mark and Loralee spent nearly an hour with the Swenson family when they went to pick up the baby.

The house was clean but filled with hints of the disarray that came with children. The tree lights twinkled, and children's Christmas music was playing. Janie offered to feed them dinner, but they were more than full from the meat loaf and potatoes they'd eaten quickly before leaving.

With plenty of instructions and a big bag of provisions, Mark and Loralee finally left with Joseph. Loralee dressed him for bed as soon as they were settled in, and she was disappointed when he drifted off to sleep with little effort. She and Mark prepared for bed as usual, each checking frequently on the baby. Since Janie had told them he usually woke up soon after midnight, they decided to watch a movie rather than trying to go to bed early. Halfway through *It's a Wonderful Life,* Joseph woke and made his presence known. They took turns holding the baby through the duration of the movie, then they turned off everything except the Christmas lights and snuggled by the tree with Joseph between them. His little eyes gazed at the lights with apparent wonder until he drifted back to sleep, and Mark and Loralee did the same.

Joseph woke again around three, and this time he wasn't so easily pacified. But between the two of them they managed to make him comfortable, and sometime after four he went back to sleep. This time, Mark and Loralee went to bed. Mark was quickly snoring, but Loralee lay awake, not feeling sleepy at all. She felt something formless awakening inside her that seemed to spring from this opportunity to spend time with this sweet little boy. She couldn't explain it, but she relished the peace that came with it. Making an early New Year's resolution to be more content with her life as it was, she finally drifted to sleep a little after five.

Joseph woke up at seven, starving and full of wiggles and cries. When his stomach was full, Mark helped Loralee bathe him in the kitchen sink, the way she remembered her sister bathing her first baby. They both ended up almost as wet as Joseph, but the laughter they shared made up for it. Mark left for a short while to feed the animals and take care of the bare necessities, then he returned, insisting it was his turn to hold Joseph.

Loralee was not as disappointed as she thought she'd be when it was time to take Joseph home. The refreshed vigor in Janie Swenson's appearance was gratifying, but it paled in comparison to her renewed joy in seeing her baby.

"Oh, how can I ever thank you?" she asked three times. "I lay down a few minutes after ten, and the next thing I knew it was past eight o'clock this morning. It was *heavenly.*"

"Glad we could help," Mark insisted.

"Thank you," Loralee told her husband as they drove toward home.

"For what?"

"For indulging me. I really enjoyed it."

"Do you think I didn't?" he laughed, pulling her hand to his lips. "You're going to make a wonderful mother," he added, meeting her eyes with affection. Loralee turned to look out the window as tears pooled in her eyes. But she had to smile. They were tears of hope.

Loralee's mood was dampened slightly when Mark

commented on the missing baby Jesus as they headed toward the door. She'd forgotten all about it, and made no comment.

An hour later, the house began to feel empty again. Loralee was just wishing for a distraction from her latest baking project when Mark came into the kitchen and leaned against the door frame. "Let's go somewhere," he said. "I feel like shopping or something."

"It's probably ridiculously crowded in town, and—"

"I don't care. We don't even have to buy anything."

"You talked me into it." Loralee quickly cleaned up the mess she'd made and grabbed her coat. She took a long glance over her shoulder as they passed the Swenson home, and she thought for several miles about how excited the children must be. Then she thought of sweet little Joseph, allowing her mind to savor the memories of holding him close. Trying to focus her thoughts on hope rather than grief, Loralee found herself imagining Joseph wrapped up tight and lying in the empty manger on her lawn. She smiled to herself at the image in her mind, and a tingling warmth bubbled up from inside her at the thought.

"Is something wrong?" Mark asked, reaching for her hand while he drove.

Loralee shook her head and smiled at him. "It's just that . . . I feel it."

"It?"

"The spirit of Christmas," she said quietly. "I've shopped, and decorated, and baked, and given parties and gifts. But I haven't been able to feel the spirit. You know . . . that indescribable feeling inside that you used

92

to get as a child."

"Yes, I know," he agreed.

"Well, I feel it," she beamed. "It's as simple as that."

"Perhaps Joseph had something to do with it," Mark observed.

"Perhaps he did," she said softly, drifting off in thought again.

They were not disappointed by the crowded parking lots and long lines they'd expected. Loralee followed Mark through a toy store, indulging him in his regular need to keep up on the latest games and Legos. He already had quite a collection at home, and occasionally he actually played with them.

For no apparent reason, they both stopped in the middle of the doll aisle. Mark turned to look at her with a quizzical expression, while at the same moment an idea jelled in her mind.

"Are you thinking what I'm thinking?" he asked as if someone might overhear.

"I don't know. What are you thinking?"

As if there was no need to clarify, they hurried to the front of the store, where they each got an empty cart. Fighting the crowds and the noise, they went up and down the aisles, selecting items while Loralee recalled aloud the things Janie had said she'd already gotten for her children. They finished by picking out some clothes and blankets for Joseph, in various sizes to give him room to grow. When they finally stopped to itemize the contents of both carts, they realized they were on the doll aisle, where they'd started. Out of nowhere, Mark said, "Let's buy one for the manger." He pointed to a selection of life-like newborn dolls.

"This one," Loralee added, picking up a box. "It reminds me of Joseph."

Mark added it to the cart and grabbed several rolls of wrapping paper on the way to the check stand. They stood in line for what seemed forever, and arrived home just before dark. Mark turned on the Christmas lights and music while Loralee gathered scissors and tape. They laughed and made a glorious mess while they wrapped the gifts, speculating over the children's reaction to their surprises. Then, with the packages bundled securely into two large, sturdy garbage bags, they drove to the Swenson home and quietly left the anonymous offering on the porch. Loralee pulled the car up the road a little and parked behind a huge tree, waiting with the headlights off. Mark knocked on the Swensons' front door and ran, hurling himself into the car before there was any sign of life on the porch. They laughed together as they drove away, confident they'd not been detected.

Mark stopped the car in front of the house, but instead of getting out, he pushed an arm around Loralee's shoulders and eased her close to him. "I love you, Mrs. Thompson," he said, kissing her cold nose, and then her lips. "We have a wonderful life ahead of us, you know."

"Yes," she said, "I know."

A light snow was beginning to fall as they went into the house, hand in hand. Loralee made another silent resolution to show more appreciation to Mark. He was so good to her that he could almost make up for not having children. She reminded herself to enjoy all they were blessed with, and not be so preoccupied with what they didn't have.

Loralee put the Christmas dinner she'd prepared earlier into the oven and set the table while Mark went out to check on the animals and settle them in for the night. She changed into a nice dress, and when Mark returned she could hear him picking up the wrapping mess they'd left in the front room. She came out to see if dinner was ready and met him in the hall.

"We forgot something," he said, handing her the baby doll. He'd taken it out of its packaging, and wrapped it tightly in a white blanket that he'd obviously gotten from a drawer in the nursery.

Without a word, they walked together outside, the doll cradled in Loralee's arms. The snow was falling harder now, and the ground was quickly disappearing beneath it. The little white lights surrounding the nativity sparkled almost magically.

Loralee hesitated next to the manger, her focus on the little doll. Though she could never explain it, something inside told her with certainty that she would be blessed with a son of her own one day. In that moment, she knew it was not a matter of *if*, but *when*. In the same thought she believed there would be difficult times ahead, and perhaps more disappointment. But in her heart she *knew* it would happen.

Feeling nothing but peace and joy, Loralee moved to place the doll in the soft bed of straw. She wondered why Mark gasped, but only an instant before she gasped herself. Lying in the manger was their baby Jesus—the one Mark's grandfather had made so many years ago. It glowed with a fresh coat of paint, intricate with life-like details, covered with a protective coating that would spare it from the elements. Tucked next to the baby's head was a little note. Mark picked it up and read with a chuckle: "Next year, we'll kidnap Mary."

Mark laughed toward the sky and hugged Loralee tightly. "I can't believe it," she said. "Who would do something so . . . sweet?"

"I don't think it matters, my love," he replied. "It would seem we're not the only mischievous ones out and about tonight."

Loralee laughed and admired the baby Jesus once more before they returned to the house and shook off the snow. Christmas lights and the smell of baking ham with cloves met their senses. A quiet rendition of *O Little Town of Bethlehem* played on the stereo.

"What do we do with this?" Loralee asked, handing the baby doll to Mark. He looked at it a moment, then took it into the nursery. Loralee followed and watched him lay it tenderly in the center of the crib. He covered it gently with the blanket Joseph had slept under, then he put his arms around Loralee and held her tightly. That warm tingling encompassed her again as her ears tuned in to the lyrics floating from the other room.

How silently, how silently the wondrous gift is given!

So God imparts to human hearts the blessings of his heaven.

"One day . . ." Mark said, and Loralee believed him.

About the Author

Anita Stansfield is an imaginative and prolific writer whose four published novels have been outstanding successes in the LDS romance market. She has been writing since she was in high school, and her work has appeared in *Cosmopolitan* and other publications. She is an active member of the League of Utah Writers.

Anita and her husband, Vince, live with their four children in Orem, Utah.